dog eat dog

MODERN
African
Writing
from Ohio University Press

This new series brings the best African writing to an international audience. These groundbreaking novels, memoirs, and other literary works showcase the most talented writers of the African continent. The series will also feature works of significant historical and literary value translated into English for the first time. Moderately priced, the books chosen for the series are well crafted, original, and ideally suited for African studies classes, world literature classes, or any reader looking for compelling voices of diverse African perspectives.

Welcome to Our Hillbrow: A Novel of Postapartheid South Africa
by Phaswane Mpe
ISBN: 978-0-8214-1962-5

Dog Eat Dog: A Novel
by Niq Mhlongo
ISBN: 978-0-8214-1994-6

After Tears: A Novel
by Niq Mhlongo
ISBN: 978-0-8214-1984-7

From Sleep Unbound
by Andrée Chedid
ISBN: 978-0-8040-0837-2

On Black Sisters Street: A Novel
by Chika Unigwe
ISBN: 978-0-8214-1992-2

Paper Sons and Daughters: Growing Up Chinese in South Africa
by Ufrieda Ho
ISBN: 978-0-8214-2020-1

The Conscript: A Novel of Libya's Anticolonial War
by Gebreyesus Hailu, translated by Ghirmai Negash
ISBN: 978-0-8214-2023-2

dog eat dog

NIQ MHLONGO

OHIO UNIVERSITY PRESS
ATHENS

Ohio University Press, Athens, Ohio 45701
www.ohioswallow.com

First published by Kwela Books,
a division of NB Publishers,
40 Heerengracht, Cape Town, South Africa
PO Box 6525, Roggebaai, 8012, South Africa
http://www.kwela.com

First published in North America 2012 by Ohio University
Press

Printed in the United States of America
Ohio University Press books are printed on acid-free paper ∞ ™

20 19 18 17 16 15 14 13 12   5 4 3 2 1

First edition 2004

Library of Congress Cataloging-in-Publication Data
Mhlongo, Nicholas.
  Dog eat dog / Niq Mhlongo. — 1st ed.
    p. cm. — (Modern African writing)
  ISBN 978-0-8214-1994-6 (pbk. : acid-free paper) — ISBN
978-0-8214-4413-9 (electronic)
  1. College students—Fiction. 2. City and town life—Fiction.
3. Johannesburg (South Africa)—Fiction. 4. South Africa—
Fiction. I. Title.
  PR9369.4.M48D64 2012
  823'.92—dc23
                                        2012016750

To Lily Morobane
for giving me all the support that I needed.

one

Dear Mr Njomane

The University of the Witwatersrand Bursary Committee acknowledges that it has received your application for a bursary dated the 4th of March.

We regret to inform you that your application was unsuccessful.

We have looked carefully at your application letter and based our decision on the information that you have supplied. Unfortunately you did not meet the criteria set by this Committee.

We wish you every success in your future academic endeavours.

Kind regards

Dr Jane Winterburn
Chairperson and registrar:
The University Bursary Committee

I received that curt, insensitive letter on the warm evening of the 13th of March 1994. I had just eaten my dinner at the YMCA in Braamfontein. The Y, as we affectionately called it, had offered me temporary accommodation for about a month now, while I tried to sort out my disagreement with the University Bursary Committee.

I got up off my bed and opened the drawer where I had put my other two 'we regret' letters. As if to make sure of their meaning, I unfolded each one and read it again. The wording was the same except for the dates. *Did anybody even read my applications?* I wondered angrily. I thought I had supplied everything that the Bursary Committee needed: copies of my father's death certificate and my mother's pension slip, an affidavit sworn at our local police station giving the names and ages of the nine other family members who depended on my mother's pension, as well as three other affidavits confirming all movable and immovable property that we owned. Although, unfortunately, my family did not own any immovable property as the house in Soweto that we had been living in since 1963 was leased to us by the apartheid government for a period of 99 years. *What more information do these people want about the poverty that my family is living in?* I asked myself.

Anger smouldered inside me as I read the letter again. *Why did the committee have to be so polite in dismissing my application?* They should have told me plainly, 'We regret to inform you that you are black, stupid and poor; therefore we can not waste our money on your thick Bantu skull.' I could have swallowed the words if they were simple and direct.

Now the thought of being forced to part with the cheese life of the Y because of this letter from the Bursary Committee was like a curse. It was as cruel as a man who chops off the breasts of the mother as the hungry baby tries to suck the fresh milk from them.

Did this mean I would be forced to hook up again with those

hopeless drunken friends of mine? Was I going back to that life of wolf-whistling the ladies who passed by in the street, calling them izifebe (prostitutes) if they did not respond the way we liked? I felt like I was being pushed back into a gorge filled with hungry crocodiles.

There was nothing exciting for me about living the life of the unemployed and unemployable, whose days in the township fold without hope. I thought I had said goodbye to cleaning the dog shit out of our small garden. I didn't want to go back to waking up early every Tuesday morning to stand outside with the rubbish bag in my hands, waiting for the garbage truck. I was completely bored of watching the predictable soapies on my brother's television set just to kill the slow-moving time. I was tired of my uneventful township life as a whole.

That month that I had been allowed to stay at the Y I had tasted the cheese life. I had my own room, and although I was sharing it with my newly acquired friend Dworkin at least I enjoyed some privacy, unlike at home in our four-roomed Soweto house.

At home I still slept in the dining-sitting room although I was twenty years old. Yes, at home I was woken up at four o'clock in the morning by the footsteps of my two brothers on their way to the kitchen to boil water before they went to work.

I was happy at the Y. I had almost forgotten the smell of sewage that filled the air at home each time the chain jammed in the cistern of our small toilet, which was outside in the right-hand corner of our 25-square-metre yard. I was enjoying the luxury of using the soft and freely supplied toilet paper; the skill of softening pages from a telephone directory when answering the call of nature in the township was no longer necessary.

At the Y I could differentiate between my meals. I didn't have to queue in our local shop to buy those oily, constipating fatcakes every morning. I was fed with cornflakes, bacon and eggs and Jungle Oats. I no longer walked the streets of the township to find funerals at which to get my weekend lunches. I no longer had to short-change my aunt by buying a fifteen rand piece of meat at our local butcher each time she sent me out with a twenty rand note; there was no need for that kind of pocket money anymore.

To suspend the pain and frustration that was sharpening inside me I inserted a Peter Gabriel cassette into my tape recorder, and the song *Don't Give Up* started bellowing from the speakers.

Don't give up
'Cos you have friends
Don't give up
You're not beaten yet

The lyrics reminded me of how my father used to encourage me when I ran out of faith. My old man would tell me that to keep on trying would never kill a man. That was the sort of advice that I needed, as I looked deep into my mind for the solution to my problem. I was never going to give up trying.

two

On Monday morning I stormed into the Financial Aid Office at the East Campus Senate House. I just couldn't understand why I could not be granted some kind of financial assistance. The government was pumping large sums of money into the Universities for needy black students like myself. I deserved that money.

I had already made up my mind about what I was going to say to the secretary. I was going to tell her that I wanted to have a word with Jane. Jane was the first name of Dr Winterburn, who wrote me those three insensitive letters. I didn't know her and I had never spoken to her before. I did not even know where her office was. All I knew was that if you want to get past a stubborn secretary to have a word with their lazy boss, you need to use the boss's first name. That is the only way, to make them to think that you know their boss from somewhere or that you are in some way related to them. Otherwise the secretary will tell you that the boss is unavailable, or in some endless meeting. They will dismiss you even if the boss is available, but doesn't want to be disturbed while surfing the Internet for child pornography.

I marched towards the counter, avoiding the three-metre-long queue. I had already told myself that I was not going to stand in that queue. Enough was enough. I had spent too long dusting those benches with my arse while waiting in vain for that bursary. I had nothing to lose. The decision not to grant me financial assistance had already been taken. *I will show them today*, I said to myself as I reached the counter.

As I expected, I was immediately subjected to a barrage of insults from a coloured secretary with a narrow forehead. She made sure that everyone inside the office could hear her.

'Shoo! You know I thought they lie. But they were right to say that if you want to hide money from a black person, you must put it in writing,' she said rubbing her temple with a yellow ball-point pen.

There was some laughter from the students in the queue behind me.

'What do you want in the university if you can not read?' She looked at me with disdain. 'Can't you see what is written there?' she said, pointing at the sign on the white wall.

Straight-faced, I slowly turned my head and read the sign.

STAND IN THE QUEUE AND WAIT FOR SOMEONE TO HELP YOU

I paused for rumination. I was seething with anger.

'Bullshit! What does a bimbo like you think I want? Gold?'

I heard a sigh of awe from the other students in the queue.

'Get out of this office at once!' shouted the secretary.

'Nice try. But you can only chase me out if this is your uncle's office.'

'This guy! Who the hell do you think you are to speak to me like that?'

Without thinking I answered. 'I'm Jesus from heaven.'

The sound of laughter came from nearby. 'Whoever you are, what makes you think you are more deserving than the rest of these people who are standing in line?'

The office became silent as all eyes were turned on me. I didn't care; all I wanted was an explanation as to how on earth they thought I would raise the money to study without a bursary. Meanwhile my enemy had disappeared into the office next door to call her supervisor.

'Is this the one, Rachel?' asked the overweight woman, pointing to me as if I was a witch.

'Ja Ms Steenkamp,' replied the one with the narrow forehead.

Ms Steenkamp folded her arms boastfully, as if she was the Governor of the Reserve Bank. She shot me a shrewd look and raised her nose as if she was confronted with a disgusting township rubbish dump. Her malicious bloodshot eyes locked with mine as she pointed her short, fat forefinger at me and began in a commanding tone of voice.

'Hey you! If you need to be helped in this office you need to behave like the other students. Do not storm in here like you are entering a butchery or supermarket.'

There was more laughter from everyone in the office. She paused and waited for the laughter to subside.

'Haa! Just look at him! Do you think this is Cuba? Do you see Fidel Castro here? Do you think you can just get a free education without standing in the line like the others?'

Encouraged by the laughter as well as my silence, she continued:

'You must act like a civilised person and apologise to Rachel for your apish behaviour. Then you must stand at the back of the line if you want to be helped in this office. Otherwise you will not receive any money from us,' she said, dismissing me with a curt gesture using the back of her hand. It was a gesture that an angry owner uses to dismiss his troublesome dog.

I did not know what to say. My mind was clouded. I could not think properly. I tried to open my mouth to say something but my lips seemed tightly sealed, as if they were glued together.

With sudden energy I vented my anger, thumping the counter with a loud bang. Most of the files and papers that were on the counter fell down as a result. The coloured secretary Rachel and her overweight boss Ms Steenkamp lurched back, waiting to see what my next move would be. I began to swear, my voice building to a scream:

'F-f-f-ffuu-ck!'

That was all I could think to say to her at that moment. The way everyone looked at me, I guess nobody had ever said such a swearword in that office before. A moment of silence fell. I had lost my temper. I didn't care anymore.

'Nne-ver, ee-ver, I mean never ever ee-ever speak to me like that. Do you f-ffucken understand me, you fat bitch?'

I have no idea where those words came from. Neither did I understand what they meant at the time. I didn't even notice that two black security officers had been called and were standing right beside me. They were holding their knobkerries, but I couldn't stop. The two security officers had arrived at the wrong time, when my anger was at its peak. I was not afraid of them, come what may.

'Do y-you know who you are f-ffucking with?' I moved back and forth like a heavyweight boxer who is ready to throw another punch. With my right fist I thumped hard on the counter. 'I mean do you ugly fat ladies know who the f-ffuck I am? Do you want to lose your f-ffucken jobs because of what you have just f-ffucken said? Hhee?'

'Ho! Ho! Please relax man. Insults are not worth it man. I understand you are angry,' said the black security officer who was trying to calm me down. 'But you are talking to ladies, remember?'

I turned to the security officer. 'Just shut up! I'm not f-ffucken talking to you,' I said, pointing my forefinger at him.

There wasn't another word from him. I turned back to Ms Steenkamp.

'Do you want to regret having seen me in this office today?'

I paused and looked at the two ladies as if I was waiting for an answer. They were bloody scared. I opened my eyes wide as if the two ladies had just insulted the president of the country. My aim was to frighten them into thinking that I was some big name. *They must think I'm the son of their employer, although their employer is probably white,* I convinced myself.

Everyone was watching me; I guess most of the people were trying to think where they might have seen me. Some of them must have thought for sure that I was the son of the Minister of Finance, or cousin of the President, or some important celebrity. But before I could vomit more insults, a white lady entered through the main door. She approached the counter, obviously surprised at the sight of the two security guards. Something in my enemies' body language told me that somebody important had arrived.

'My Gawd! What is going on here?' she exclaimed. 'I'm Dr Winterburn, the registrar in this office.' She paused. 'Is there some problem in this office I should know about?'

I felt that I had to answer her before anybody else took advantage of the situation. I summoned all my courage to dispel the anger that was already clouding my mind, and said as calmly as I could:

'This lady here called me an ape when I came to see Registrar Winterburn, and I demand to lodge a formal complaint to her sup . . .'

Before I could finish my sentence the secretary with the narrow forehead interrupted me.

'Ja. You think you're clever mos. Say what you were saying before. Come on say it now. Tell her.'

'Never shout and point at me like that,' I warned her.

'Let's not be emotional and . . .' said Dr Winterburn, looking at me.

'Who's emotional?' I snapped.

'I mean, it's natural to be emotional and I understand how you feel,' she said patronizingly.

Her attitude made my blood boil.

'Listen here! Are you coming to take sides or have you taken them already?'

'No no no. We don't take sides in this office,' she countered defensively. That's where I wanted her, on the defensive. 'I'm only trying to find out what happened because I'm the one in charge here. Please don't misunderstand me.'

'OK then. These two ladies insulted me by calling me an ape.'

The two secretaries hissed as I tried to explain, but Dr Winterburn shushed them.

'Ms Steenkamp, is it true that you called this man an ape?' she asked, trying hard to be fair.

Ms Steenkamp gave a little derisive laugh, her eyes blinking in disbelief. 'No! Jeez! Good heavens!' she exclaimed. 'I did not call him an ape.' She paused. 'I was called by Rachel to come and talk to this guy who was forcing his way into the office instead of standing like the other students in the line and waiting for somebody to help him.' She paused with her finger still pointing at the queue. 'So I said to him he should stop his apish behavior. My God! I can't believe this!'

Ms Steenkamp tried hard to make herself look more innocent.

'You see! That's what I don't appreciate,' I said, feigning horror. Like lightning, I flicked my eyes from Ms Steenkamp to Dr Winterburn. 'And she is repeating it right in front of you, saying that my behaviour is apish. That is like saying that I was socialised with apes and I should be living in the mountains or the zoo. Is that what you see when you look at a black person like me?'

'Bullshit! That is not true. I didn't . . .' said Rachel.

'What did you say just now?' I snapped again.

Silence fell while Dr Winterburn considered our statements. The look on her face told me that she was siding with me.

'Rachel, what happened before you called Ms Steenkamp?' enquired Dr Winterburn.

'This gentleman came straight over to the counter and I had to tell him to go back to the end of the line. When he refused to do so I had to call Ms Steenkamp.'

Like a judge in a court of law, Dr Winterburn turned and faced me. 'And why did you refuse to follow those procedural orders?'

'Dr Winterburn, I know all about the procedures here.' I paused. 'For me to make an appointment to see you in this office all I need

16

to do is sign a form which is inside those files.' I paused again and pointed at the files, which had been picked up off the floor by one of the security guards. 'And not to stand in the queue with the other students.'

I paused and looked at Dr Winterburn. She was nodding in agreement. 'I was coming to do just that when these two ladies here tried to embarrass me in front of all these students. This one even took the piss out of me by asking me what I was doing at university if I could not read the signs.' I pointed at Rachel. 'She said that without even greeting me properly, let alone asking me what I wanted like any civilised person would. That is not the way to treat people. They are here to help the students, not to insult us.'

'He's lying. Ask the officers. He's the one who swore in this office!' shouted Rachel.

None of the security officers came to her rescue. Maybe they were siding with their black brother. Rachel was breathing hard and her eyes were beginning to mist over with tears. Dr Winterburn turned and faced the two officers who were leaning on the counter, listening to everything that was being said.

'Gentlemen, I think I can handle this little misunderstanding on my own.'

As soon as the two officers had left, Dr Winterburn invited Ms Steenkamp, Rachel, and myself into her office. She ushered us into the chairs and the three of us sat nervously in anticipation of her verdict, while secretly observing each other.

'Sorry, I didn't get your name,' Dr Winterburn said, trying to address me in a conciliatory tone.

'I'm Dingamanzi Makhedama Njomane,' I answered.

My two enemies remained anxious and silent.

'Mr Njomane, as you might have heard I am the one in charge here.' She paused. 'It's against the policy of this institution as a whole to insult people, or rather to make people feel insulted. I take this opportunity to apologise to you on behalf of this office, and I hope my staff will do the same.'

The breath whooshed out of me in disbelief. I did not expect the matter to be concluded with such simplicity. Both my enemies looked at Dr Winterburn in disbelief and tried to mask their disappointment by remaining silent. But with a look that no one was likely to disobey, Dr Winterburn turned to the two ladies to elicit their apologies.

'I'm sorry if you took my words to imply what you thought. It was not my intention to insult you,' said Ms Steenkamp reluctantly.

'I'm also sorry for the misunderstanding that happened between us. I hope you did not take it that bad. I did not mean what you imply,' muttered Rachel quickly.

'Okay. Thank you. You two can leave us now,' ordered Dr Winterburn.

I watched my enemies leave the office with glee. But I knew that a mammoth battle was still ahead of me.

Without a word Dr Winterburn opened the top drawer in her desk and took out a diary. She hunched forward and removed her glasses, pushed her long bushy red hair backwards with her right hand, and then began to page through the diary with her long fingers. She groped in the same drawer again and took out a small brown bottle, from which she took two pills. She poured a glass of water from a carafe on the table, put the pills in her mouth and swallowed them with some water.

For about a minute Dr Winterburn scrawled something in her diary. I became mesmerised by the trick that age had played on her once fresh flesh. Although her body showed that she was still young, her face revealed wrinkles that were the result of the unstoppable wheel of time. I started to wonder if she still dated at her age. In my perverted thoughts I began asking myself if she enjoyed spreading her legs for ambitious gigolos to dance between. Looking at the thick make-up on her face, I concluded that she was that type who would share her nakedness with young white men, under the illusion that their pace between her thighs would keep her forever young.

I didn't notice that Dr Winterburn had finished scrawling in her diary. I was stroking my chin in deep erotic thought when she closed it and spoke to me.

'Okay Mr Njomane, what is it that you came to see me about?'

'About the status of my bursary application.'

'Do you have your student card with you?' she asked as she re-set her PC.

I reached for my wallet in the back pocket of my jeans, took out the card and gave it to her. She typed something into her PC and drew back, waiting for the information to appear. By that time I had begun to sweat. Dr Winterburn leaned forward and folded her arms. She exhaled heavily and leaned backwards again.

'I thought that you already knew the outcome of your appeal, Mr Njomane. I wrote to you early last week. Haven't you received my letter yet?'

'Yes, I received your letter, but the grounds on which I was re-fused the bursary are Greek to me. I came here to make an ap-pointment to talk to you about it.'

'What do you mean?' she asked, her face flushing with aston-ishment. 'Are you here to tell us what to do and what not to do?' She looked at me and hunched forward again as if she was talking to a deaf person. 'Look here, Mr Njomane; in this office we have our own criteria for selecting students for bursaries. Remember we would love to sponsor everyone who asks for help, but we are circumscribed by the funds we have at our disposal. There are quite a number of students whose situation is really pathetic and we have decided that in your case at least it is not that bad.'

Dr Winterburn hunched forward again and looked at me. She balanced her elbows on the table. I did not say a word.

'What I suggest you do is to apply for outside donors. You can get a list of addresses from Rachel, our secretary.'

I bit my lip in disappointment.

'To begin with, Dr Winterburn, I came here to understand what you actually mean by saying that my situation is not that bad. It seems that you people in this office have got the wrong end of the stick about my situation and . . .'

'What's your point, Mr Njomane?' she interrupted.

'My point is this. I got an exemption two years ago and I have been sitting at home since then waiting for the opportunity to study at this institution. I applied to the Faculty of Arts and got admitted to do my BA. It's my wish that this office grant me a bursary so that I can study, graduate, get a better job and assist my poverty-stricken family. My father has passed away and my mother is a pensioner and single-handedly supports nine members of our family. There's nowhere I can go for help except this office.'

I took out my brown envelope. It contained my father's death certificate and my mother's pension slip as well as the three affidavits.

'This is the second time that I have submitted this evidence and I wonder if the committee took any notice of it when it reached its decision,' I added as I pushed the documents towards her.

Dr Winterburn took the documents and a pause followed as she pretended to be studying them closely.

'That affidavit shows that twelve family members live crammed into a four-roomed matchbox house in Soweto.'

She started looking for something in the bottom drawer. Her other hand was rubbing at the corners of her bloodshot eyes. I knew she was looking for her glasses. From where I was sitting I could see them; they were buried under an avalanche of documents that were lying on her desk, including some of my documents. She found them without too much effort, put them on and began to study my documents.

'Mmm, so how does your family survive on your mother's three hundred and fifty rand pension?' she asked, pushing my documents away.

'It's really difficult. Our electricity and water have been cut off because the bills have not been paid for the past two years,' I lied.

20

I was not ashamed that I lied. Living in this South Africa of ours you have to master the art of lying in order to survive. As she looked at me I hid my hands under the edge of the table so that she couldn't see my gold-plated Pulsar watch, which I had bought the previous year at American Swiss.

I looked Dr Winterburn straight in the eye. With her left hand she pulled open the bottom drawer, took out a packet of Consulates and a lighter. Next to the carafe was an ashtray filled with butts and half-smoked cigarettes. She carefully balanced a cigarette between her lips, then paused and watched the yellow flame of the lighter flicker between her fingers.

'This is your first time at this university, isn't it?'

'Yes ma'am,' I answered.

She took two deep drags on her cigarette and then flicked the ash sharply into the ashtray. 'Oh, I see,' she said.

three

Dr Winterburn read each one of my documents carefully. At the same time she added some information to the notes on her computer screen. I glared at my father's death certificate, which lay next to her right hand.

Raw memories of the past surged through my mind. I remembered my sister and myself paying my father a visit in hospital the day before his death. I wasn't young, I was doing my standard nine. I remember to this day my father lying in his hospital bed. He had seemed unusually small like a child; there were dark shadows under his eyes and his skin was very pale, so pale in fact that I could actually count the veins underneath it. He could not even move on his own.

I looked at my sister. Her eyes were filled with sorrow and as she stood in the corner of the hospital room she began to sob. But I was brave enough to stand closer to my father; I wanted him to die in my arms.

Maybe we have turned into strangers to him, I thought with pain when my father showed no sign of recognising us. But later he called out my name. He raised his hand and I held it. He even said something faintly, but I couldn't hear him. I called his name softly a couple of times, and unconsciously he kept saying 'hmm' each time I repeated it. He got tired quickly and closed his eyes. I rested his hands on his chest as the nurse arrived and told us it was the end of visiting time.

The following day I heard that my father was gone. That was the first day that I knew fear existed inside me. I did not go to school that Monday. How could I, with that unspeakable sense of grief?

When I finally went to school three days later the Big Punisher, as we called him, was waiting to discipline me for my truancy. That morning, after the assembly and prayer, the names of the truants were read out and they were called upon to appear in the disciplinary room. My name was on the list.

The deep-mouthed Big Punisher was smiling as I stood in front of him. 'Son, those who live in glass houses must not throw stones; obey our rules or face punishment. You know that being absent for a day is ten strokes of the cane. You have been absent for three days so you must multiply that by three,' he said, mercilessly straightening his cane.

When I didn't say a word he continued: 'Do you want to take your punishment in instalments or all at the same time, son?' He let out a small malicious laugh. 'Come on, son. If you take it cash at the same time I will give you a discount of five,' he said, as if we were completing a business transaction.

When I still did not answer he ordered me to bend over and receive my punishment. 'I know you will be able to talk after five of the best.'

The pain that I had felt when Big Punisher punished me the previous week, for fluffing my lines when I was called upon to recite the theorem of Pythagoras, resurfaced. I recalled bitterly how he had made my hand bleed with that thick cane while I screamed for mercy. To this day I can still see those scars when I take a bath.

'Oh no. I have a valid reason for not coming to sc . . .' I began, but he would not even let me finish my sentence.

'Eh, eh. No, no, no, no,' he said, shaking his head. 'No excuses, so don't piss in the wind and waste my time.' He put his fat index fingers in his ears. 'I've heard a lot of stupid reasons today. Enough is enough.'

He started to list every reason that he considered stupid.

'My mother was delivering my baby brother so I had to help spread her legs. My philanderous father's dick was swollen from

23

the syphilis he caught over the libidinal weekend so he sent me out to buy him some VD pills. My younger sister broke her virginity the day before yesterday and her punana was leaking blood, so I had to help my lazy mother wash her sheets and cook for the family. My brother was castrated by a mob over the weekend after being accused of sleeping with a jailbait.'

I knew that the Big Punisher had an orgasm every time he inflicted pain. He had beaten me several times before. I also hated mathematics, which was the subject that he was licensed to teach with only a standard ten. He had once punished me severely for scoring nine percent in algebra. Because of that he gave me nine strokes of the cane. According to him I was good at mathematics, but just too lazy to practice it. I had consoled myself that day because a friend of mine called David was given ten strokes of the cane because he had got ninety percent. The Big Punisher said that if it weren't for his laziness he would have got one hundred percent. After that we all concluded that he was mad after all.

There was a tall table next to where I was standing. He ordered me to bend over and put my head underneath it.

'But Sir . . .' I tried to talk but the words would not come out of my mouth. Instead I started to cry.

'Tears don't scare me my boy,' he said harshly. 'If you were that afraid of the cane you should have played by the rules. Is it asking too much from you to come to school every day?'

After five of the best I couldn't take any more. I attempted to flinch away from the advancing cane but only succeeded in banging my head severely on the table.

'We are not calling it a day yet. There are five more rounds to go boy if you decide to take it in installments,' he said, laughing maliciously. 'I told you that after five horizontal ones you will decide whether to take it cash or instalments, didn't I? And if beating you here on the school premises isn't to your liking then I will do so in front of your father after school at your home, boy.'

The mention of my father fueled the agony inside me. Suddenly something snapped and I shouted.

24

'You will never hit me again in your life, you son of a bitch!'

The Big Punisher was very surprised to hear those disrespectful words. He started rolling up the sleeves of his shirt.

'What did you say to me boy?'

I did not answer. I could not believe I had just insulted him like that. He continued rolling up the sleeves of his blue shirt.

'I'm going to teach you how to behave and how to talk to your elders. I can see that you have big balls and want to prove it to me in a fistfight, boy. A cane is not good enough for you,' he said as he started to loosen the tie around his neck.

He put the tie down on the table and undid the top button of his shirt. 'You talk too much, boy. I will teach you people today.'

Surreptitiously I sized him up. I was just sixteen years old with bum fluff. He was a forty-year-old family man with a potbelly.

While he was still relaxed and sure that he would teach me a lesson, I gathered all the power that I could summon and punched him as hard as I could. My right fist thumped into his dark bloated face and floored him. His glasses broke and the glass scattered all over the floor. I picked up the fan that was on the table to finish him off, but somebody grabbed me from behind.

'Stop it at once!' It was the voice of my English teacher, Mrs Magwaza. She was standing behind me holding my arm.

The Big Punisher was still on the floor. Like a police dog, he was sniffing and spitting. Blood oozed from his mouth. Very slowly he raised himself up and started picking up the remnants of his glasses.

'I'll find you. I'm coming to your home tonight, boy!' he shouted angrily, spitting blood.

'What happened?' asked Mrs Magwaza.

But I did not answer her. I pointed at Big Punisher with my forefinger.

'I'm not finished with you either.'

Big Punisher was very angry. He broke loose from two teachers who were trying to restrain him. Seeing that he had overpowered them, I scurried out of the disciplinary room and ran outside in the direction of the rockery between the two long classrooms. Pupils started peeping through the windows. Some stood in the doorways so that they didn't miss out on the action. I could hear Big Punisher breathing heavily a few metres behind me as I ran for my life. I ran to the rockery and picked up one of the cement blocks that had been used to build it. At very close range I flung it at Big Punisher. The block hit him straight in the face. He fell down and started kicking for his life.

I was very scared. Mrs Magwaza came running, screaming at the other teachers to call an ambulance. Instead, the school gardener came running with a hosepipe and sprayed water over Big Punisher. I stood at a safe distance, wondering whether I had murdered my teacher at the age of sixteen.

The following day I did not go to school. It was a busy day at home as we were preparing for my father's funeral. I hadn't told anybody about what had happened at school.

Around three o'clock in the afternoon I saw Mrs Magwaza's car coming down the road towards our home. I sensed trouble and as it drew nearer I went to the outside toilet and pretended I was busy in there. I peeped through the crack of the door and saw Mrs Magwaza, Big Punisher and three more of my teachers emerge from the car. They entered our house through the kitchen door.

After gathering some courage I came out of the loo and went into the house after my teachers. There were about fourteen people in our dining-room; they had all come to pay their last respects to my father. The teachers were already seated when I came in. It must have become obvious to them that somebody had passed away. I could tell that their minds were smudged with unspoken thoughts, but I greeted each one of them, including the Big Punisher, as if nothing had happened. His left eye was completely closed and there was also a big gash between his eyes that was stitched together with some black thread. He was holding a pair of sunglasses in his right hand.

Big Punisher and my brother knew each other from high school. I made sure that I sat with them to monitor the atmosphere. Everybody in the house looked sad. No one seemed to have noticed the wound on Big Punisher's face. Sitting next to him was my biology teacher. He had punished me once for using a picture of a naked girl that I had cut out from my brother's *Scope* magazine to decorate my biology exercise book. He was a very close friend of Big Punisher; I knew that they used to drink beer together. I also knew that he bore a grudge against me because I had been delivering flirtatious messages on behalf of my cousin to the schoolgirl he was chatting up at our school. *He will do anything to fabricate lies that would corroborate those of Big Punisher about my bad behaviour,* I thought nervously.

After a while my brother started introducing my teachers to my aunt. 'Aunt Ntombi, this is my friend Jerry. I went to school with him.'

There was a little pause after my brother had pointed out Big Punisher as everybody in the house turned to look. My brother continued: 'These are his colleagues and they are all Dingz's teachers.'

'It's a beautiful thing to know that the straight and narrow can still be traced among the youth of today,' my aunt began in a dispirited voice. 'In our days life was communal. When one family cut its finger, the rest of us bled. When a neighbour's house was on fire we would bring water. Today is different because folkways have been sidelined with all this so-called modernity. When a person dies a friend will come and demand payment of his unpaid bills. It is very rare and a pleasant surprise to see you young people still upholding the spirit of ubuntu by coming to pay your last respects to the deceased. Ubuntu is the invincible gold of human companionship. It is a perfect product of nature and the basis of the society. With your presence here today, you have shown

27

the Njomane family that education is not only limited to the knowledge of books, but goes beyond that to include the building of character.'

There was a moment of silence. My teachers glanced at one another. They were nodding at my knowledgeable aunt, but I was not convinced that they were there to extend their condolences. I knew that the Big Punisher was there to give me the beating he had promised me in front of my father, but unfortunately for him my father was no longer in this world to witness it.

'So when did this misfortune happen?' Big Punisher and my English teacher asked simultaneously.

'It happened last week, but we decided that Dingz should not come to school until yesterday as he was very upset,' answered my brother.

My teachers looked at each other for a short while. They didn't know what to say. *Their mission has failed,* I thought happily. Somehow they would have to say that I had told them about my father's death. Otherwise why had they come to our house? Were they there to rub salt into the wound? Or were they there to pass their heartfelt condolences? *No, they won't let our big secret out now,* I convinced myself.

'Yeah,' Mrs Magwaza started hesitantly, 'that is why we have all come – to offer our condolences.'

After an hour or so my teachers left. My brother and I took them to their car – I wanted to make sure that they didn't mention anything about our fight.

'We didn't get to talk Jerry; what happened to your eye?' asked my brother as they were about to get inside the car.

'Oh this? It's nothing,' said Big Punisher. 'I had a little car accident. Don't worry, I'm fine.'

'When did it happen?'

'The day before yesterday.'

'So how's your car?'

'Not that bad.'

As he answered my brother's questions I noticed that he was lisping. I watched him closely to assess the damage for myself and saw a wide gap where his two upper front teeth had been knocked out. The other teachers were already inside the car. Big Punisher got into the back seat and my brother closed the door for him.

'Don't forget to come to school on Monday. We have a test on Tuesday.' It was Mrs Magwaza reminding me. 'Ask David your friend about specific chapters we are going to write about.'

'Yes, Mam.'

It was over. I had won.

four

Landing back in Dr Winterburn's office from the reminiscence of my father's death, I saw her putting my documents back into the large brown envelope that I had brought with me. She took a deep breath and sighed. She looked at me, back to her computer and then to the ceiling.

'Mr Njomane, the decision was taken on the basis of the information that we had at that time. But I'll try to use my influence to get the committee to reverse their decision. You will hear from us in writing within the week.'

'Thanks very much,' I said.

'Not so fast, Mr Njomane. Remember I'm not promising anything.'

'Yes, Dr Winterburn.'

'All right. For now you must leave these documents with me.'

I felt relieved. I hoped that something positive was going to come out of this nightmare. I thanked Dr Winterburn for her patience and left.

But before I could get far, I suddenly felt a sharp pain in my gut. It was as if someone had stabbed my stomach with a sharp razor blade and cut my intestines. It was the kind of pain that I imagine Verwoerd felt the day Tsafendas's knife intruded violently into his gut.

As I entered the toilet I saw three guys standing and pointing their penises towards the gutter. I passed them and went straight to the basin, where I turned on the tap and washed my hands, I splashed the water over my face and onto my shaven head.

The mirror that was attached to the wall above the basin reflected a very different face from the one I knew as my own. The pimple on my forehead had turned into a little tumour. My eyes were round and bloodshot.

The pain began again as I left the mirror. I pushed open a cubicle door that was ajar. The door hit the knees of the person who was sitting on the toilet inside.

'Somebody. Gee! Don't you knock when opening a closed door?' said an anonymous voice.

I didn't answer. I went straight to the next cubicle, after convincing myself that there was nobody inside. Closing the door behind me, I took down my pants and sat on the toilet. I tried to force something out of my stomach, but it would not come. It was already twenty past eleven – I had missed an African Literature tutorial. But I hadn't prepared for it anyway. I would attend the next class, which was Political Studies, at twelve.

I sat there inside the ceramic shitpot thinking about my victory. As I relaxed, staring at the ceiling, I felt something coming out of my bowels. I tried to push but it went back into my colon again. I tried again with all my power, but only succeeded in emitting a very loud fart. The guy next door started to laugh. Those who were urinating at the gutter joined him. The laughter continued. I didn't care; they couldn't see my face anyway. I lingered inside the cubicle, waiting until they had gone. Suddenly there was a knock on my door.

'Somebody,' I answered.

'Are you shitting or masturbating?'

'Both. Do you want to eat my shit or drink my sperm?'

'Uhhu! Shit! That smells. What did you eat?'

'Your sister.'

'Shit. It's stinking.'

'Of course it is. Did you expect a beautiful aroma?'

It was quiet for a little while, then there were footsteps: somebody was coming into the toilet. I heard the door to the cubicle on my left being closed; then I heard laughter.

'What are you laughing at?' I asked.

31

'Nothing. I'm just thinking of your mother.'

I kept quiet and stared at the wall. On the white door next to the handle there were some words scrawled in black highlighter:

DON'T JUST SIT THERE AND BROOD LIKE A CHICKEN!
SHIT LIKE THUNDER!

I immediately remembered what my brother's educated friend had said when I had been back home in Orlando West the other day. He had encouraged me to read any graffiti, whether good or bad, wherever it was written. He said I would always learn something from it. Even when I took a piece of newspaper to wipe my arse after having a shit, I should read it. According to him, this would make me knowledgeable. I didn't know whether that was good or bad advice; your guess would be as good as mine. But that was the reason I continued to read the graffiti. Many things were written there. The graffiti on my left-hand side really amused me:

IF YOU WANT YOUR BIG DICK TO BE
SUCKED WITHIN A MINUTE,
PUT IT THROUGH THE HOLE ON YOUR RIGHT
AND YOU WON'T REGRET

A second lot of graffiti, which complemented the first, read:

WIPE YOUR BUTT
AND PUT IT AGAINST THE HOLE ON YOUR RIGHT
FOR A FREE RIDE

I looked to my right and saw a small hole stuffed with some toilet paper. The hole was big enough for a penis of my size to fit through. Somebody with a sick mind had bored through the thin ceramic tiles separating the two cubicles. What amused me was that the hole was embellished with blackish ink, like pubic hair on a vagina. I tried to stop myself from laughing but to no avail. Suddenly I heard an anonymous voice from next door.

'What are you laughing at?'

'I'm imagining me and your mother fucking tonight.'

'Fuck you.'

'You too.'

'You must be a mad guy.'

'Maybe. But I remember your mother telling me that she was pregnant with you about nineteen years ago.'

'You wish, motherfucker.'

I heard the toilet flushing. Then there was a very loud bang on my door.

'I think you are trying to shit to gain a light complexion. Good luck, black boy.'

I heard the main door to the toilet open. Before my anonymous friend could leave I swore loudly: 'Fuck you too.'

It was now eleven forty-five. I took out the toilet paper that was blocking the hole on my right, and peeped through the hole to convince myself that there was nobody there. I stood up, wiped my arse, and lifted my penis towards the hole. But before my glans reached the hole I hesitated. *What if somebody is waiting to suck my dick on the other side? What if they cut my glans?* I heard footsteps. Somebody was coming. I withdrew my penis and zipped up my jeans. Outside the cubicle, I washed my hands and dried them. I looked in the mirror again. I had a lecture in five minutes time. I had to go. Time up.

five

At about half past three that afternoon I found myself at the Jorissen Street branch of the Standard Bank. The sun was still very hot. There were about nine people waiting to use the ATM. Ahead of us was a middle-aged black lady who was busy having her private conversation with the ATM. By the way she looked around her, it seemed to me that there was no agreement reached between them.

A thick red line on the pavement that bore the warning **STAND BEHIND THIS RED LINE** separated her from the short, moustached black man behind her.

About four or five minutes passed. The black lady stood inert in front of the ATM. Her card was still in the slot and I could hear a beeping sound as she looked around her.

'Oh boy! What is she still doing there?' said the blonde behind me to herself.

Making sure that nobody is watching her, or else blaming herself for putting her money in the bank instead of under her mattress, I answered her silently.

The black lady at the ATM looked around again. The blonde curled her lip. She started cursing impatiently each time the black lady inserted her card into the slot to redo her transaction. Agitated, she ruffled her thatch of long blonde hair with her manicured fingers and began tapping her right foot on the pavement.

I looked her up and down; her red dress stashed away her beautiful slender body from shoulder to hip, leaving her sunburnt legs naked. Stylish sunglasses were pushed up into her blonde hair.

At long last the cursing blonde exploded. 'Excuse me. Do you mind helping her? She seems to be struggling,' she pleaded, pointing at the lady at the ATM.

What she didn't realise is that I had a lot on my mind. I was not in a good mood at all. My meeting with Dr Winterburn had taken its toll, and on top of that I had just received the grade for my first Political Studies essay and I had failed it.

With a sudden flash I turned and looked at the blonde. Anger was building up inside me. *Why pick me when there are three people in front of me?* I asked myself angrily. She could have even offered to help the lady herself if she was really serious about it. *Why me? Is it because she is used to blacks running her errands every day?*

'Is it because I'm black?' I asked.

With a shade of disbelief creeping into her voice the blonde responded, 'Jeez! I was only sayi . . .'

Her face turned pale from my insinuation. Her long blonde hair wagged about as if she was looking for a hole in the ground to swallow her up immediately.

I could tell that my words had had a strong impact. Yes, it is true that I was implying that she was a racist. It was the season of change when everyone was trying hard to disown apartheid, but to me the colour white was synonymous with the word and I didn't regret what I had said to the blonde.

Anyway, I had been told that playing the race card is a good strategy for silencing those whites who still think they are more intelligent than black people. Even in parliament it was often used. When the white political parties questioned the black parties they would be reminded of their past atrocities even if their questions were legitimate. Then the white political parties would have to divert from their original questions and apologize for their past deeds.

The blonde looked around her to see if anybody had overheard our nasty little conversation. People remained unaware of what had passed between us. I stood with a scowl on my face, anticipating her response. She finally summoned up enough courage to speak and stammering said:

35

'My gosh! Why on earth do you think I'm racist? I was just . . .'

'Because you are white,' I answered.

'So that qualifies . . .'

'Yes. I know the likes of you and I'm sick and tired of pretending. When you see a black man like me I know you don't see a man, but a black boy.'

'I'm sorry if you feel that way. I was merely saying that maybe she would be more comfortable being assisted by you.'

I clicked my tongue. 'Ag! Voetsek maan! What made you think she would be comfortable being helped by me and not you or anybody else in this queue, including the security officer over there?'

'Oh jeez, I mean . . .'

'Yeah. It's because I'm black just like her, isn't it? And you think you are different from us,' I snapped.

The blonde made some attempt to absolve herself but I turned to face the ATM. The security officer had helped the black lady and I was now second in the queue.

When my turn came to use the ATM I found I had three hundred and thirty rand in my bank account. I withdrew three hundred rand and headed to the nearby Moosa Supermarket to buy some groceries. As I walked away I could feel the blonde's eyes on my back.

Themba, one of my township friends, had finally got a job as a cashier at the Moosa Supermarket. From the shelves I took as many goodies as I wanted without even bothering to check their prices. At the till Themba would either pass my goodies through without ringing them up, or he would ring up a lesser price. As he was doing this he would say, 'The rand is weak my friend, we must save money when we have a chance'.

The total that flashed up on the cash register was forty-seven rand and eighty-one cents. The groceries that I had filched were worth more than one hundred and eighty rand.

In order to hoodwink the shop manager, who was sitting at the other till, I tendered eighty rand in tens and twenties. Themba then gave me more than thirty rand in coins. At the door was a black security officer, I folded a ten rand note and handed it to him underneath my receipt; he smiled at me and ticked the receipt.

Along the way back to the Y and not very far from the Moosa Supermarket was a bottlestore. The change that Themba had given me at the supermarket was jangling in the back pocket of my jeans. I walked inside with my grocery bags and within a few seconds I had increased my load by twelve cold beers.

At the corner of De Korte and a small street that I didn't know the name of, I started feeling the weight of the heavy plastic bags that I was carrying. My fingers began to twitch as if I had cut off the blood supply.

I stopped by the robots opposite Damelin College to see if there was a car coming. There was nothing on the road, so I crossed before the green man appeared on the robot and sat down on a big stone under a giant tree next to the College building. I looked inside one of my bags and saw some appetising biltong curling up at me like a snake.

I put my hand inside the plastic bag to pull out the biltong. But instead I touched the ice-cold Black Label dumpies. My mouth started to water. I tried to swallow the saliva, but my throat was too dry. I spat out the saliva and watched the blob fall noisily on the tarmac while my hand groped inside the bag again. With a mind of its own, my hand bypassed the biltong and came out with an ice-cold lager. I laughed at myself, but I didn't put the beer back in the bag. *After all, the Y is still far away and I am tired of walking. Who's going to see that I'm drinking a beer under this tree?*

As I twisted the top off my dumpie my mind landed comfortably on the very first glass of beer that my father gave me. That was way back in the late 1970s.

My father was a good musician. Unfortunately none of his chil-

37

dren took after him, but in drinking I think I outclass my old man. My mother used to complain a lot about my father's drinking and his late homecomings; sometimes she would even accuse him of having an affair. But later I found out that my father was just enjoying playing his music and drinking beer at the bottlestore, where he could find good drunken backing vocalists to accompany him when he played his Xizambi.

This traditional Shangaan instrument was made out of a thin cane which was bent into the shape of a bow. A melodious string would be fastened from one bent end of the wood to another. A short carved stick would then be struck against the cane, providing percussion and melody at the same time.

My father was brilliant at carving and he used to make his own instruments as well as other things. He would often go to the countryside and fell trees from which he would carve wooden spoons, wooden plates and things for home decoration. He would sell those things for profit at the train stations during his spare time.

Most of my father's followers were drunken women that he met at the bottlestore. Every Friday night we would hear him coming from afar with the crowd behind him singing along in carefree tones. But by the time he reached our home the crowd would have disappeared. His food would be ready on his carved wooden plate, but he would continue playing his instrument. Sometimes he would ask my mother to join him in a tune. She would join in if she was in a good mood. She knew all of his songs. He sang the songs when he was both happy and sad, or when he wanted to make a point about something.

There was a particular song that my father used to sing when he wanted to tell a troublesome tenant to leave our home. Its Shangaan title was *Nghoma ya makhalibode*, *The song of cardboard boxes*, and it went like this:

Ayi gube ya makhalibode	(Take your cardboard boxes and leave my house)
I khale mi hi nyagatsa	(It is long that you been troubling us)
Aho chava ku mi hlongola	(We were afraid of chucking you out)
Hi nghoma ya makhalibode	(This is the song of the cardboard boxes)

After singing that song we all knew that someone among my father's tenants should leave the house, but my father was a very kind man and although most of the tenants in our home were our relatives, they never paid rent.

One day my father arrived home late, singing as usual. My mother was very angry because he had spent most of his money on beer. What made matters worse was that earlier the same day she had come home with her hand torn and bleeding. She and her friends had been bitten by the dogs at a farm near Pimville. A white farmer had set the dogs on them as they were trying to collect cow dung to smear on the floor of our house. Only one of her friends managed to escape, by jumping the fence. My mother was caught by the arm by one of the dogs, while her other friend was caught by the leg. After enjoying their plight the farmer instructed his dogs to leave the 'kaffirs' alone, but the scar is still vivid even today. My father used this as an opportunity to compose a song about white people. The song ran as follows and was in English:

You white man leave my family alone
This is the last warning
I worked hard and paid lobola for my wife
Unlike you who just give them a ring to put on their finger
I have eight children with her not just two

But that night we were woken up by a serious argument in my parents' bedroom. My brother and I were sleeping in the sitting-dining-room. We listened very quietly. My mother was threatening to leave the house because my father didn't spend enough time at home. But soon he apologized and everything was back to normal again.

The following day, a Friday, he came straight home from work sober. After dinner he told me to come with him. I didn't ask where. We went to the local bottlestore, and that was the day he gave me my very first beer. The first ever glass of beer in my life. When we came back home I was his backing vocalist. I was drunk, but my mother was happy and never complained when he took me with him. It was clear to her that if he took me with him he was just enjoying drinking at the bottlestore and not seeing other women.

I began to think about our life in Soweto in those days. At midnight every Tuesday and Friday the white policemen would knock rudely on our kitchen and sitting-dining-room doors. Without search warrants, they would rummage through our house for so-called illegal immigrants from the homelands and any other illegal stuff such as homemade ntakunyisa beer. After opening the doors, they would count us in their attempt to control the African birth rate, or influx from rural areas, or whatever the reason was.

One day my uncle, who had recently arrived from the rural areas to look for a job in the big city of gold, got a seventy-two-hour order from the police. That meant that he had to leave Johannesburg and go back to the country if he did not find a job within three days. No one was allowed to hang around in town without written permission from his or her employer in those days.

It had been about three weeks since he got the order on his urban permit document. He should have left the city and returned to the homelands a long time ago. My uncle had been surviving the police raids by hiding under a big steel bath which we would turn over with him underneath it when we heard the terrifying knock of the police at the door.

The police caught my uncle one cold Saturday night. We were still listening to a radio broadcast when they knocked. Everybody was excited by the news that Prime Minister B.J. Vorster had resigned as the Prime Minister of the country and P.W. Botha had taken over as the new Prime Minister. I was the only one who was listening with blithe indifference, as I was still politically naive. The police had been clever because they had changed their timetable and come to our house on a Saturday. But we still identified the knock at the door as theirs because it was very loud as usual, and was followed by the words, 'Polisie, maak oop,' spoken in a gruff voice.

In two ticks my uncle had run to the kitchen to take his usual shelter. Unfortunately for him the steel bath was full of soaking clothes. There was no way he could throw the clothes out because the water would spill all over the place and make the police suspicious. Sweating, my uncle just stood there in nervous anticipation of his fate.

Suddenly the voice at the door became unfriendly.

'What are you natives still doing there? Do you think we have the whole night for you? We will break this scrap door now!'

We all froze with horror inside the house. We were aware that the police were capable of doing what they said – they had broken two of our doors the year before because we had not responded in time. The first time they came was around midnight when we were all asleep. My father was still getting dressed when they said he was wasting their time and broke down the door. The second occasion we delayed them, as we were still hiding my uncle under the steel bath. Because of this our small bedroom, where three of my brothers and my uncle slept, had no door as we had used it to replace the sitting-dining-room door. A sheet had been hung across the doorway as a substitute for the broken door.

I heard my mother pleading with the policemen in the dark.

'Please don't break, I'm coming now,' she said, struggling to unlock the door, which was already being pushed hard from outside. As she opened it, it whipped open and banged against her forehead. Stolidly she stepped aside for the four uniformed white policemen and their two black colleagues to enter.

'What were you doing inside, woman? Still making babies? You natives! Next time we will break the door and beat you up for delaying us,' shouted one of the tall officers, as if my mother was deaf.

The officer flashed an electric torch into my mother's eyes and dazzled her.

'Let me see your permit.'

Without a word she quickly went to her bedroom and returned with a written page. The officer used his torch to complement the dim light from the single candle in the corner. In an effort to aid the police officers, my mother went inside her bedroom again to get a lamp, which was made out of a small Royal Baking Powder tin.

By the time she returned we were all in the sitting-dining-room waiting to be counted like animals in the kraal. I was still drowsy, because even though my brothers were listening to the radio I had been slumbering.

Two police officers started counting us and the other four ferreted around in every corner of the house.

'You are supposed to be ten in this house. Which baboon does not belong here?' asked one of the police officers angrily.

We were all afraid to point a finger at my uncle. My parents looked down. My brothers and I looked at my uncle. He was very scared. But I heard his quivering voice.

'Me, baas.'

'Where are your papers?' asked another police officer.

Before my uncle could respond, the police officer's fat hand was on the scruff of his neck. I was hoping that they wouldn't beat him up; Brixton police were notorious for their violence.

There had even been rumours in the township of the appearance of a feared whites-only police squad. We kids were made to believe that they had more than two thirds of their faces covered by a bushy beard and moustache, and because of this you couldn't see their mouths when they were silent. According to the rumours, in order to speak the Brixton whites-only squad would hold their bushy moustaches up with their left hands and pull down their beards with their right to enable them to open their mouths. It was also believed that they would walk around with small brooms to help them sweep their bushy wrist thatches out of the way when they wanted to check the time on their watches.

I stood in the middle of the room stupidly, examining each police officer in an attempt to verify this rumour. Meanwhile my uncle was handing his expired papers to them.

'You suppose to have been gone to the country by now. You go with us today, boy.'

'Please sir, don't . . .' pleaded my mother.

'Shut the fuck up! You kaffir bitch!'

Silence fell. We watched in horror as my uncle hobbled helplessly out into the street with the police. They all disappeared inside the police van and I only saw him again ten years later.

six

The sweet kwaito music blaring from a white CITI Golf passing along De Korte Street helped to bring me back from my reminiscence. I looked at the time. It was ten minutes to six in the evening. The gliding amber of the sun was sloping down to usher in the evening.

I searched the pockets of my jeans and took out the packet of Peter Stuyvesant that I had just bought at the supermarket and unsealed it. I lit a cigarette and inhaled the stress-relieving smoke.

When I had finished I threw the butt into the road and took out my Walkman. I pressed the play button and began to listen to Bayete. The name of the song was *Mbombela*. I lifted my bottle of beer; it was almost half-empty.

When I raised my eyes from the beer bottle, the police car had already stopped in front of me. I hadn't heard them arrive because of the fat beats coming from my Walkman. I pulled the earphones off and let them dangle around my neck.

At first I thought that they wanted some smokes, but then I realised that the police officers had caught me with an open beer. In two ticks both front car doors were flung open and I shrank like a child caught masturbating by its single mother as they moved hastily to accost me.

'Evening, sir.'

'Evening.'

'How are you, sir?'

'I'm alright.'

'Enjoying yourself, hey?'

'Yep.'

'Do you realise that what you're doing is against the law?'

'Excuse me? You mean relaxing under this tree?'

'No. I'm talking about public drinking.'

'I'm not drinking anything.'

'The evidence is in your hand.'

I looked at the bottle that I was still holding. I never expected policemen to be patrolling that quiet street. I thought that they would be attending to more serious crimes elsewhere. But there they were, spoiling the party that I was beginning to enjoy with my other self. *Why can't these people just leave a person to do his own thing?* I asked myself. I moved my eyes away from the bottle and looked at the pimple-faced Indian police officer.

'I'm just holding an open beer bottle that I was drinking when I was in the bar, sir. But I'm not drinking it now. And if that's a crime I didn't know.'

'We stopped the car because we saw you drinking, my friend. Do you think we're stupid?'

Silence fell while I looked at his tall, white, moustached colleague, who was mercilessly chewing some gum. He staggered forward and I could tell from his bulging bloodshot eyes that he was already drunk. His face was also bright red, as if he had lain in the sun for too long, and the golden hair on his skull stood up like a scrubbing-brush.

'Are you denying that we saw you drinking?' asked the red-faced officer.

'It is just a misunderstanding, sir; I wasn't drinking this beer.'

'Ohh! You think you're clever, né?' the red-faced officer asked contemptuously. He leaned forward and shook his large head slowly as if he was feeling sorry for me.

'What is your name?'

'Dingz.'

'Are you a student?'

'Yep.'

'Where?'

'Wits.'

He studied my face for a while. When he started to talk again, his words were accompanied by the heavy smell of liquor and cigarettes.

'OK. Listen, Dingz. We have been asked to patrol this area because lately there have been complaints about students who abuse alcohol. They drink and throw the empty bottles into the street and that's not good for the environment. Look there!' he said pointing at some empty Coca-Cola cans on the other side of the road. 'Is that not disgusting?'

'So what does that have to do with me?'

'You say you're a student?'

I nodded.

'And you're holding a beer?'

'But I'm not one of those students you are looking for. If you'll excuse me gentlemen, I have to go.'

I thought I had succeeded in talking myself out of trouble, but before I could even raise myself from the ground the red-faced officer asked me yet another question.

'What are you doing at Wits?' he asked, sprinkling my face with saliva.

'Law,' I lied. 'Why?'

I thought that maybe then they would leave me alone, but the white officer continued looking at me; he was sizing me up. Then the Indian officer started to lecture me in a patronising tone of voice.

'I wonder if you're aware that a student was arrested last week on a charge like this one. Fortunately he was not doing law.' He paused and gave me a sympathetic look. 'I understand you guys studying law are not allowed to take legal job if you have been convicted of a criminal offence. It would be bad for you if we take you in now.'

I was realising the seriousness of my situation. I started to reflect on my future; all my efforts to get a place at varsity would prove futile if I was arrested now. *Oh shit! Me and my drinking!*

The white officer was nodding along to everything his friend was saying. I remained silent, but they could see that they had managed to scare me. The white officer leaned closer to me. 'Listen! Here is a deal, pal.' He lowered his tone to a confidential whisper. 'Either you come with us now to spend three months in a prison cell, or face a one thousand rand fine . . .' He paused and looked at my reaction. I kept my cool. 'Or we can sort this thing out right now, out of court, by reaching a gentlemen's agreement.' A pause again. 'Which means you can stop our mouths with only seventy rand, my friend.'

The Indian officer was nodding to support what his colleague was saying as I debated with my other self about the best step to take. I had never been in jail before. I had only heard scanty rumours about the Big Fives, the Twenty-Sixes, Apollos and other prison gangs that sodomise and kill other inmates. But at that moment I was more worried about my family at home. *What will they say if they learn that I was arrested for public drinking?*

There was a moment of silence between the two corrupt officers and myself. Then the red-faced officer bent over and grabbed my beer bottle and two of my grocery bags. He was mumbling something in Afrikaans. The other officer grabbed me by the scruff of my neck and picked up my other plastic bag with the sealed beers inside.

'It seems my friend it is that time again, when you have the right to remain stupid and silent because everything that you say can be used against you in court.'

'Whaa! I can't believe how some people can be stupid. We gave you a chance my friend and you blew it. Boom!' said the Indian officer.

They opened the rear door of the police car and pushed me inside with my grocery bags. The walkie-talkie inside the car started belching and cutting. The red-faced officer retrieved it and muttered something in Afrikaans as they got inside and started the engine.

By then I realised that I had messed up my chances of buying myself out. I still had about one hundred and fifty rand that I had taken out at the ATM that afternoon. I knew that the officers would try everything to incriminate me. *They are used to the system. They are also the ones who corrupt it. They know how it works and how to exploit it in their favour. Even if it means that I sleep in a cell just for one night for my disrespect, it would please them.*

The earphones that were lying on my shoulders were still blasting music. I groped inside my pocket in an attempt to find the stop button on my Walkman. I was familiar with the buttons because I had owned my Walkman for the past four years, but suddenly I changed my mind about switching the music off. I opted just to rewind the tape. I found the button I was looking for and rewound the tape.

The car hadn't moved even five metres when I began to plead with them to stop. 'I'm terribly sorry, officers. I don't want to go to jail. I think I have eighty rand for you.'

The red-faced officer smiled and stopped the car.

'Now you talking sense.'

Pleasant smiles broke quietly on their lips as I searched my pockets for my wallet. I unzipped it and handed them four twenty-rand banknotes, money that my mother sacrificed from her pension every month to help me through my cashless varsity life.

The two officers looked at each other and took the cash. I groped inside my pocket again to reach the play and record buttons on my Walkman. Simultaneously, I pressed the two buttons down. Then very politely, in a friendly tone as if I was admitting my guilt, I asked them, 'Are you sure that you'll be fine with only eighty rand? I have a feeling that this is a very serious offence?'

'You're right. You can add more if you have it. But do not make the same mistake again next time. OK, my friend?' said the white officer.

'I won't.'

I looked at the nametags on the pockets of their blue police shirts.

'Sergeant Naicker and Sergeant Viljoen, I'm terribly sorry for the inconvenience that I've caused you. Because of my behaviour I will add twenty rand just to apologise.'

I offered them another twenty-rand note. Sergeant Naicker took it. He smiled at me and said. 'Ja. If it wasn't for Sergeant Viljoen we would have taken you in today.'

'You're a really lucky bastard, my friend. Do you know that? This is what we call being clever. Ask Sergeant Naicker here. We normally fine people two hundred rand for a case like this. We just thought that you are a poor student and decided to fine you less, my friend.'

'Hmm! Are you sure a hundred is fine because I can add another twenty.'

'Just give us another ten and disappear. One hundred and ten from a student who cares about his future is fine. The next time you're in trouble you must call us or come straight to our police station along this road. You know the station, mos? Ask to speak to either Sergeant Viljoen or Sergeant Naicker here and you'll be safe.'

'Thanks a lot.'

The engine was running and the right indicator light was flickering. I opened my rear door to leave.

'Sorry we can't drive you to your place. We are in a hurry for an emergency in Hillbrow. I'm sure you can manage.'

I took my grocery bags out of the car and closed the door behind me. The car moved slowly to join the flow of traffic heading for the CBD. I stood on the pavement and began to wave goodbye. Then suddenly I signaled at them to stop the car, as if I had forgotten something inside. I put my grocery bags down and approached the driver's door, while they both looked at the back seat to see if there was something I had left there. I took my Walkman out of my pocket; the record and play buttons on it were still pressed down, and the red record light was flickering. I showed it to Sergeant Viljoen.

'What now?' he asked, perplexed.

'Are you stupid? Can't you see that our conversation is recorded on this cassette?'

'Shit! You fucking bastard! You will pay for this.'

'Hey! Mind your language, Sergeant Viljoen! This thing is still recording.'

'F-fuck!' swore Sergeant Naicker from the other side.

'He's only trying to scare us. There's nothing there,' said Viljoen to console his colleague.

'Suit yourselves, I'll see you in court then.'

I turned my back and pretended I was leaving, but before I could go very far they called me back. 'Hey you! Come here, you.'

Within the blink of an eye the two officers were out of the car. I thought they were going to negotiate a deal with me, but that was not the case. Suddenly Naicker's big hand was around my balls and I was standing on my toes with pain. Viljoen grabbed the Walkman from my pocket. I tried to resist, but Viljoen's fist struck me across my mouth. I tasted blood. Naicker let go of my balls and I staggered and fell down. I lay still on the pavement pretending I had lost consciousness, but Viljoen's boot struck me in the ribs. A few minutes later I was handcuffed and bundled inside the car.

'Never fuck with the police again, my boy,' warned Viljoen as the car turned past Hillbrow Hospital.

I didn't have the nerve to utter even a single word. I looked at my grocery bags on the floor of the car next to my legs. The brick of butter that I had bought had melted and was almost flat. One of us must have stepped on it. The bottle of mayonnaise had been broken and there was the smell of it inside the car.

At Esselen Street the car turned to the right in the direction of Berea. Ahead of us were about half a dozen police vans with flickering lights parked next to a tall block of flats. The handcuffs

were very tight and I felt like the blood wasn't circulating properly in my hands. I looked at the time on the dashboard. It was already twenty minutes past seven in the evening. I had missed
my dinner at the Y.

'These things are too tight, please loosen them,' I pleaded.

'That serves you right, boy,' said Naicker as the car came to a
standstill next to the other police vans.

There were lots of people standing around. All eyes were on
the block of flats. Policemen were all over the place with sniffer
dogs. Naicker and Viljoen got out of the car without saying a
word to me, locked the doors and walked towards the entrance.

After about an hour some policemen came down through the
door with some guys who were handcuffed. Deep in my heart I
was hoping that Naicker and Viljoen were amongst them, but
they weren't. I sat there wondering what the guys might have
done. They had probably been arrested for a much more serious
offence than mine. I looked at my plastic bag again and spotted
the Black Label. *No more drinking*, I told myself.

At about ten minutes to ten, I spotted Viljoen coming towards
the car. He opened the driver's door and sat inside. 'Where do
you stay?' he asked.

'YMCA,' I answered.

Without asking my permission he opened one of my Black
Label dumpies. He drank about half of it without taking a break
and gave a loud disgusting belch. 'Do you want some?' he asked,
as if he was going to give me the one that he was holding in his
hand.

I nodded, but all that I really wanted was for him to set my
hands free. In a while I saw Naicker coming towards the car as
well; he stopped in the middle of the road and lit a cigarette. Viljoen put the bottle on the dashboard and searched his pockets. He
took out some keys and unlocked my handcuffs. Naicker opened
the front door and within seconds we were on our way back in
the direction of Braamfontein. Viljoen tossed a cold beer to me

and I twisted the bottle open. Naicker offered me a cigarette, but I found it too difficult to smoke with my swollen lips.

At half past ten they dropped me at the entrance of the Y with my plastic bags. My ribs were still very painful. My front teeth were loose and my left eye was nearly shut. I had lost my Walkman, my beers and my money.

seven

Yea, though I walk through the valley of the shadow of death I fear no evil

I lay on my single bed, under the full glare of a dazzling bulb reflected from the white ceiling, reading the sticker on the door of my wardrobe. The ink had faded away on the third line and all that was legible were the words '*Psalms*' and '*David*'. But I knew from my religious education at primary school that the words were taken from the Good Book, Psalm 23 of King David. We used to be forced by our teachers to memorise the psalms that were prescribed in our Bantu (Blacks Are Nothing To Us) syllabus. Because of that my head is still heavy and addled with the psalms like a traveller's jumbled suitcase.

I was alone in my room at the Y as my roommate Dworkin hadn't come back the previous evening. I guessed he was out jolling, as ladies were never allowed in the residence except those employed by the Y authorities to do the laundry for us.

I had woken up at five o'clock that morning and taken a long warm bath. Since I knew that I was naturally not an early riser I had arranged with Dunga the day before to come and wake me up at half past six. We had planned to be at the Braamfontein Civic Centre by seven o'clock to vote. But that morning I didn't need Dunga to wake me, I was too excited about voting for the first time.

By half-past six I was getting more and more impatient. I thought that if we left immediately, as arranged, we would arrive there earlier than everyone as it was only about five minutes' walk from the Y to the Braamfontein Civic Centre.

In order to kill time while I waited for Dunga I was finishing off the last chapter of *Animal Farm* by George Orwell. I still enjoyed the story although I can't recall how many times I had read it previously. It had been one of my favourite prescribed novels when I was still doing standard nine in the late 1980s. As I read I could hear a Zulu struggle song being sung outside my window.

UMandela uthimay'hlom'	(Mandela says let the warriors get ready)
Yebo may'hlom'	(Yes let's get ready)
USisulu uthimay'hlomihla sele	(Sisulu says let the warriors be ready for the battle)
UDe Klerk asimfun'	(We don't want De Klerk)
Yebo asimfun'	(Yes we don't want him)
Siyaya. Wemkhonto we sizwe epitori, yebo may'mhlome	(We're going. You the spear of the nation in Pretoria, yes let's be ready for the battle)

There was the sound of whistling and the rhythmic beat of clapping hands and stamping feet from the crowd coming down Rissik Street. They were on their way to the Civic Centre.

'Bopha, comrades! Stop, comrades!' shouted a voice from the crowd, probably the leader.

Phansi ngo De Klerk phansi!	(Down with De Klerk down!)
Phansi!	(Down!)
Phansi ngo De Klerk phansi!	
Phansi!	
Phambili ngoMandela phambili!	(Forward with Mandela forward!)
Phambili!	
Phambili ngoMandela phambili!	
Phambili!	

54

Phambili ngomzabalazo phambili!	(Forward with the struggle forward!)
Phambili!	
Phambili ngomzabalazo phambili!	
Phambili!	
Viva ANC Viva!	
Phansi ngamabunu phansi!	(Down with the whites down!)
Amandla!	(Power!)
Awethu!	(To the people!)

I was watching the crowd and enjoying the rhythm from my window. The crowd passed and I walked towards the white bookshelf that was mounted on the wall. I put the copy of *Animal Farm* on top of my other books: Amah's *The Beautyful Ones Are Not Yet Born*, *Down Second Avenue* by Prof Es'kia Mphahlele, Richard Wright's *Black Boy* and Steve Biko's *I Write What I Like* and many others.

I sat back down on my bed and began to remember how, when I was at primary school, my teachers used to rely on me to perform poetry for our parents during functions such as parents' day, and during the visits by the school inspector. Because of my ability to memorise words, I was often asked to stand before a crowd and entertain them by reciting poetry from our school syllabus. *All Things Bright and Beautiful* was my favourite English poem. For Afrikaans I used to do *Muskiete Jag*, though I only found out the meaning of the poem when I was in high school. Luckily, it was recited to our parents, who didn't really understand what was going on. However, after each performance the performer would be praised for having a good command of the language by the assembled parents.

Before each performance took place we would practise each step of the performance under the supervision of our English teacher until he was satisfied that we were ready to appear on stage. Even to this day I still remember each gesture to *All Things Bright and Beautiful*. For example, where it says 'All creatures great and small' we were taught to use our hands to indicate 'great and small'. Where the line reads 'All things wise and wonderful' we would tap our right index finger against our heads to gesture 'wise', and for the word 'wonderful' we would spread our hands wide with a smile on our lips. We would then point to the horizon with the same index finger for 'The Lord God made them all', with the palm of our left hand spread under our left breast to show our appreciation of everything that The Man Upstairs had done for us.

I remember disappointing my teachers by messing up a very important part of my performance for the school inspector. Instead of pointing my index finger at the horizon where it said 'The Lord God made them all', I knelt down and pretended to pour traditional umqombothi beer and snuff, like it's done in the ceremony for our sacred oracle. The reason I fluffed that line was because on the day before my performance at school there was a traditional thanksgiving ceremony to all the ancestors of our clan. On that day I was ordered by the clan elders to take part in our traditional rituals. They asked me because I carry our common ancestral name. The elders had given me a wand to tap lightly on the cowdung floor; at the same time I was ordered to clap my hands and call all the names of the ancestors.

I think those traditional rituals had confused me, but my teachers didn't think that was a good enough excuse, because after messing up the all-important gesture for 'All things bright and beautiful' by putting on some kind of pagan performance, I was caned severely. For a period of a week I was denied access to the charity soup that was supplied to black primary schools by the apartheid government.

I then began to think about the school sketches that I used to be part of during my high school days. I recalled playing the character of Old Major in a sketch from *Animal Farm*. My room suddenly turned into a theatre stage and I started to recite Old Major's speech from memory:

> The beasts of England,
> The beasts of Ireland,
> The beasts of every land and clime,
> Hearken to our joyful tidings
> Of the golden future times.
> Soon or late the day is coming,
> The tyrant man shall be overthrown,
> And the fruit fields of England
> Shall be trod by the beasts alone.
> Harness shall vanish from our backs,
> Cruel whips no more shall crack,
> And . . .

As I was about to start another line from the Old Major's speech, there was a loud knock at my door. Quickly, I got onto my feet and opened the door. Dunga and his girlfriend Thekwini, known to us as Theks, were standing there.

'Wola pintshi!' Dunga greeted me in township lingo.

'Heyta daar. Please come inside.'

'Hi Dingz,' said Theks.

'Hello.'

'I thought that you weren't alone because I thought I heard you talking,' said Dunga.

'Maybe it was the radio,' I answered, not wanting to show him how impatient I was to go and vote.

'OK. Are you ready then?'

'As always.'

'Let's vamoose then. Don't forget your ID.'

'Sure,' I said as I showed them out and locked my room.

eight

A winding fifty-metre queue stretched out from Braamfontein Civic Centre. We had been standing there for about two hours. The opportunity to vote had attracted many people; I saw a crowd of men and women the like of which I had never seen before. It was a queue of limitless hope. Many of us there thought this election would reshape our lives in the southern part of this unruly 'Dark Continent'.

The call to vote had drawn people from all walks of life. There were teachers and pupils, lecturers and students, sex hawkers and street vendors, business people and laymen, employed and unemployed, unemployables and hobos, secretaries and housemaids, taxi drivers and sportspeople. It was the moment that most of us had been waiting for years to experience.

I was standing behind a homeless man in the queue. I often saw him sleeping on the floor in the entrance of the Braamfontein branch of the Saambou Bank. I saw him every evening when I came back to the Y from the university library. As I joined the queue, I had been welcomed by the stench coming from his dirty body. I could easily tell that he hadn't touched water for days or even months.

None of us had wanted to stand immediately behind that man and this had become evident as we were walking to join the queue. Theks slowed her gait, bent down, and pretended to be lacing up her running shoes. When Dunga and myself slowed down to allow her to catch up with us, Theks advised us to hurry up and get in the queue. It was then left to Dunga and myself to decide who should stand immediately behind that stinking man. Although we didn't discuss it, we both hesitated to be the victim of that foul smell – until I was forced to sacrifice myself when Dunga pretended to be talking to his girlfriend.

Once in the queue, I took another look at the homeless man. His clothes looked like the best he could come up with from his impoverished wardrobe. On his left foot he was wearing an old worn-out soccer boot with flattened studs. Only the three white diagonal stripes on it told me that it was a soccer boot. It had turned cream in colour and I could only guess that it was once black because of my knowledge of the game. When I looked again at the same foot, I saw his big toe protruding through a hole. Around the toe was wrapped a worn-out greyish sock. On his right foot he was wearing what was once a white running shoe; a dusty grey shoelace that was obviously not manufactured together with the running shoe laced it up.

The queue was moving towards the entrance where the awaited activities of the day were taking place. As we approached the steps, the homeless man put his right leg up on the first step. I was still concentrating on his untidy hair when I felt a prod in my back. It was Theks; she was trying to attract my attention. I saw both Dunga and Theks covering their mouths with their hands to avoid what seemed to be unavoidable laughter. To share their joke with me, Theks simply pointed at the leg of the homeless man.

Theks continued giggling. When I looked at that leg, I initially thought that it was covered by the grey sock that I had seen wrapped around his big toe. But as I looked again I realized that it was just his dirty leg that had turned pale like a log in the sun; the stripes were where water had run down his leg the last time it was raining. I could not help but join Dunga and Theks in their laughter.

I continued examining the homeless man to figure out which part of his body was the main source of that foul smell. I looked at his dusty, greasy blue jeans and then up to the frayed arms of the red jersey that exposed his pale elbows. The man seemed unconcerned about his condition. He continued sharing a joke with his white hobo friend in English; he had a good command of the language, better than I did.

I tried to catch a glimpse of the homeless man's friend – I wanted to see if he was in the same league – but the only thing I could see of him was his untamed shoulder-length brown hair, which had some dry grass caught in it, and his down-at-heel, unpolished leather shoes. Just at that moment he turned to face his friend behind him to elaborate on a certain point that he was making, gesturing with his hands. I suddenly caught a glimpse of his bloated reddened face; his untamed beard covered almost three-quarters of his face and his long hair fell into his eyes. His teeth were dark brown and mottled with nicotine as if they had never been afforded the luxury of toothpaste. Between the thick fingers of his right hand was a hand-rolled cigarette; the pungent tobacco was of a brand that I had never smelled before, but it was good for lessening the stench that came from both of them.

I suddenly recognised him as the Snobbish Hobo. My friends and I gave him that name, as each time we came from the library during the night he would be sleeping under his peach double duvet, his head propped up on a continental pillow, on the floor outside the entrance to the OK in Braamfontein. As soon as he heard the footsteps of a person coming along the pavement he would immediately wake up and shake his Coca-Cola can with a few cents inside to beg for money. As I examined him I realised that his clothes were not as old as his friend's, although they still hadn't received a wash for ages. It was evident that he was a newly graduated hobo who had only recently been added to the endless statistics of homelessness and unemployment.

Behind Theks was a nicely dressed blind man. He was wearing a pair of dark glasses and a black suit, with a white shirt and blue tie. He was also carrying his cane. He held a white plastic bag in his left hand and was in the company of a middle-aged woman.

By now a long and winding queue had grown behind us, so long in fact that I could not even see where it ended. The queue extended behind the Braamfontein Civic Theatre and across Rissik Street.

Of course we all came there for different reasons. Our Big Brothers had promised beautiful things to those who lived a life of poverty, and I guess that the two homeless gentlemen ahead of me came to vote because of the promise of proper housing and employment. Some came to vote because of the promise of welfare grants, some because of the promise of free medical care; pensioners had come because of the promise of an increase in their grants so that it equalled that of their white counterparts.

I was standing in that queue because we had been promised access to a better education. I wanted to vote for whoever claimed to have fought tooth and nail to overthrow the apartheid government so that I now found myself admitted to a formerly whites-only institution. I felt morally obliged to return the favour to my Big Brothers. It was payback time for those who had been watching my back while I was sleeping. Now as an adult I felt that I had to recognise the Big Brothers' sacrifices.

Different political parties had mumbled their big lies to rally people to vote for them. I had not made up my mind as to which party to vote for, but I definitely wanted to see a black party in government. I didn't care that my Big Brothers were said to be still wet behind their ears when it came to running a country as big as South Africa. I would even have voted for the Jahman candidate who had vowed to legalise the dagga in his very first term as president. To me, just as long as he was black it was fine, as stupid as that.

The marshals were doing their job effectively. Many people were coming out of the polling station, their faces covered with broad smiles after taking part in the first free and fair elections in South Africa.

When I looked at my wristwatch, it was ten minutes past ten. The queue was moving faster but I was getting impatient to make my mark. Luckily Theks was busy entertaining us.

'Who do you think your two friends will vote for?'

'Which friends?' asked Dunga.

She nodded towards the two homeless men.

'The ones past Dingz.'

'Probably any party which will give them a free pair of socks,' I whispered.

We all sniggered and tried to cover our mouths to prevent attracting unnecessary attention.

'But di ngamla will probably vote for the status quo,' said Dunga.

'I doubt it,' said Theks.

'He played with his chance while he still had it and now it is our turn to rule,' I added.

'When do you think he started being homeless?' asked Dunga, chucking his chin.

'He was probably thrown out of the house by his wife,' I replied.

We were still enjoying ourselves when a hoarse voice came from behind Theks.

'Just leave the man alone, guys. His vote is his secret and so is yours.'

We all looked around to see where the unfamiliar voice had come from. To our amusement, it was the voice of the smartly dressed blind man who had been talking with the woman behind him. The woman herself was wearing a white T-shirt emblazoned with ANC colours and an identikit of a congressman all over it. We looked at each other and burst out laughing. We laughed not only at that liberal political rhetoric, but also that he had mistakenly screwed his face towards the two homeless men ahead of us as if they were the ones he was reprimanding.

I had originally thought that he wouldn't understand us because he and the woman had been talking Venda when they arrived and we were using a Jo'burg subculture lingo that was a mix of different languages. When the two homeless men turned to look behind, we decided to change the topic quickly.

A song in Sesotho exploded and ripped through the hot morning air as a crowd danced and sang their way along Rissik Street towards the Civic Centre.

Nelson Mandela!
Nelson Mandela!
Ahona otshwanang leyena   (There is nobody like him)
Oliver Tambo!
Oliver Tambo!
Ahona otshwanang leyena   (There is nobody like him)
Walter Sisulu!
Walter Sisulu!
Ahona otshwanang leyena   (There is nobody like him)
Hhuu left huu right!
Nyamazan'
Hoof! Hoof hoof!

The singing crowd attracted everybody's attention. Heavy drumbeats thundered behind their voices. It was a crowd of men, women and children carrying different banners and flags, praising the Big Brothers. There were ANC, SACP and PAC flags. It was obvious to me that even if President De Klerk were willing to give each one of them ten thousand rand just to vote for him they wouldn't have accepted it.

I could read two vivid inscriptions on those flags and banners as the crowd approached, ululating and singing:

LAND FIRST ALL SHALL FOLLOW

THE PEOPLE SHALL GOVERN

From the West Side of Braamfontein came a group of Inkatha Freedom Party supporters. They were chanting political slogans demanding self-rule for Zululand. I took my eyes from the crowd

63

as it disappeared around the corner to join the queue. I had thought about what the blind man in the queue behind Theks had just said about every vote being secret, and I felt ready to respond to him, but the crowd had already done enough. Even the woman he was with had unwittingly let that cat out of the bag; her T-shirt had given it all away. When our eyes met, the woman gave me her hide and seek smile.

By now the two homeless men in front of me were facing the queue marshal, who wanted to see if they had their identity documents bar-coded. The aroma of democracy was becoming stronger as I drew closer to casting my first-ever vote, but I was already thinking about the celebrations that were planned all over the township.

'What are you two doing after this?' I asked Dunga and Theks.

'I have a lot of work to catch up on at the office and I'll probably work my arse off the whole bloody day,' answered Dunga.

'Man. Today is a rest day and you should postpone everything,' I said.

'I know. But I have to do it. I'm snowed under.'

'And you, Theks?'

'I will go home after I've done some chores at my res. Did you have anything special in mind?' she asked.

'Not really. I'm just meeting some guys to celebrate. Everyone will be there except for people like Dunga, of course, who will be trying to win the hearts of their employers by working overtime alone.'

'It's not like that. I'm just tied up with work, that's all.'

'But you can do that tomorrow.'

'Maybe I'll catch up with you later.'

'Shall I give you a shout when I leave for home?' I asked Theks.

'Fine. Come pick me up around half twelve at my place.'

'I'll do that.'

'If I get bored in the office I might come straight to Orlando and join you guys,' said Dunga.

'That will be nice, we can con your mamazala into giving us free beers,' I added, winking at Theks.

'That's not a bad idea, because I'm broke,' said Dunga.

'You wish,' interrupted Theks. 'My mother won't give anybody free beers – I'll be there to make sure of that.'

Dunga lived in Chiawelo. Theks, who was three years younger than me, and I both came from Orlando West. Dunga had been my friend from childhood. I grew up with him in Chiawelo and we both went to the same high school. Theks had become my neighbour in Orlando West when I started living there four years earlier. Her mother ran a shebeen, selling liquor at her house to supplement her meagre pension. Theks was the fifth of her mother's eight children. All of her siblings were still living at their parent's house except for her oldest sister, who was living in sin with her lover in another neighbourhood.

Her two brothers were both unemployed. The eldest brother lived with his 'vat en sit' lover and two children in one of their back rooms. He made a living for himself by mowing other people's lawns for cash. Her other brother, Neo, was the same age as me. He had started a car wash along our street by the shops. I had helped him to scrawl several advertisements on old pieces of cardboard that we nailed on the telephone and electricity poles to attract potential customers.

Neo did his car-washing job under a small tent in front of the shop along our street. He had become popular with the motorists, particularly the teachers of the nearby school.

Theks had confided in me that she did not know her biological father. Her mother would not tell her anything about him. She had thought of the man who was the biological father of her two sisters as her own father. But he had died three years ago. Four different surnames were used in their house, with the eldest brother using a different surname from the rest of them. Theks used her mother's surname, which was Mkwanazi. She was the first from her family to have been admitted to a tertiary institution; in fact, Theks and myself had written the selection test for Wits University together. She had met Dunga a year before we went to varsity. At that time, both of us were kicking our heels at home with our matric exemption results. During one of Dunga's many visits to my new home in Orlando West, the two of them fell for each other. I also helped to spark their affair by encouraging the hesitant Theks to accept Dunga's advances, as he was a good person and my best friend.

Meanwhile, Dunga had graduated the previous year with a B Juris degree from the University of the North (Turfloop). He was two years older than I was and had started serving his articles at the Blackheath law firm downtown in February. When I failed to get an exemption at my first attempt in standard ten, he had passed his. I think the reason Dunga got his matric exemption in 1990 when most of us failed was his determination to become a lawyer. His mother, who was a nurse at Baragwanath Hospital, encouraged him, and while we were sitting at home celebrating the release of political prisoners, Dunga often went to the Lenasia library to study. He also didn't involve himself much in the student protests that came with angry slogans like 'pass one – pass all' which some of us thought were the perfect way to get our exemptions. Because of that belief I had to go back and redo my matric the following year in order to get an exemption.

Dunga's father had disappeared in the early 1970s when he was only a year old and it was still a mystery as to whether he was alive or dead. The authorities refused to presume him dead without any evidence, so his mother was still married to his ghost.

nine

UNEMPLOYED. FIVE DEPENDANTS: TWO EPILEPTIC,
ONE ASTHMATIC. WIFE HAS CANCER. HOUSE REPOSSESSED.
NO FOOD. NO SHELTER. PLEASE HELP. GOD BLESS YOU.

A tall dirty-looking white man was standing on Jorissen Street next to the robots. In both hands he carried a large piece of cardboard with these words emblazoned in black lettering. He waved it as he walked from one motorist to another as they came to a halt at the red light.

One kind white motorist driving a Honda Ballade called to him just as the green light flashed. He flung a coin at the man's hands, but the coin missed and rolled towards the gutter that ran along the side of the road. The man remained standing at the barrier waiting for the traffic to clear. His eyes desperately searched for the coin, which had finally come to rest against some garbage on the side of the road. But it seemed he couldn't see it, because dropped his board and anxiously covered his head with his arms. I guess he thought it had rolled into the drain.

I had picked Theks up at her Sunnyside residence on the East Campus at half-past twelve as we had arranged; I had been lucky enough to find her waiting for me. We now found ourselves jostling against the crowd in Jorissen Street, trying to get to the Jo'burg CBD to catch a taxi home. Most shops were closed, but there were still lots of people in the street.

Theks had a pile of books and since I wasn't carrying anything, I helped Theks to carry some of her load. I had declared a total abstinence from books that day; there was no reason for me to

67

study. I wouldn't have time anyway. I was going to party until the cops came knocking.

As soon as the green man appeared on the robots, Theks and I crossed to the other side. In the middle of the road we were confronted by a woman balancing a hellishly hot mbawula stove on her head. It was made out of a twenty-litre oil drum. Separating her head and the mbawula stove was a thick plank and some pieces of cloth. In her hand was a sack of mielies that were fresh from the field and ready to be roasted. But what struck me most was that the child she was carrying on her back seemed to be unconcerned by the heat and was busy sucking on a mielie husk.

'Shoo! If hell is as hot as that mbawula I will have to start preparing for an alternative place like the heaven,' I said to Theks jokingly.

'What are you waiting for?' she asked, looking at the woman. 'You must start now.'

I still don't believe that there is a being called Satan. My mother has tried unsuccessfully to convince me of his existence. But despite the fact that I don't believe in him I remain scared of those pictures of that black brute with his wriggling tail. He doesn't look friendly at all.

At the same time I think the world of that handsomely bearded hunk called Jesus. My mother loves him very much. Other pictures on our dining-room wall can be swapped and changed at any time, but my mother and my aunt would never allow us to remove that of the heavenly hunk. Every evening when my aunt says grace she directs her thanksgiving towards that picture. Every time I come back home with an excess of alcohol in my bloodstream, but still manage to open the door, the first thing I look at is that picture, just to confirm that I'm home. Without it I'm convinced that I'd be lost.

The homeless white man was standing at the side of the street by the drain. He had picked up his coin from the motorist and was examining it as if to make sure it was not a counterfeit. As we came closer I recognized him as the same Snobbish Hobo who had been standing in front of me in the queue that morning at the poll station. He looked at Theks and myself with an avuncular smile. Theks smiled back. She stopped and reached for her purse in the pocket of her tight blue jeans. She opened the purse and, taking out a handful of silver coins, emptied them into the man's Coca-Cola can.

'Girl, what are you doing?' I protested in a low voice. 'Those coins would buy us three quarts of beer.'

'I wouldn't waste my money on alcohol when I don't even drink,' she said while looking at me seriously. 'If you consider my kind gesture a waste, so be it.'

The homeless man heard nothing of our conversation. He thanked Theks for her kindness. But as we were about to leave someone behind us began to yell at the homeless man.

'You fucken white bastard Verwoerd boy! I warned you not to accept money here because this is not your fucken workplace. Come on; bring that money you have just unlawfully collected before I shave that dirty hair of yours with a warm klap. Hurry up before I take the whole tin, you motherfucker!'

Simultaneously we looked behind us. It was the black homeless man who had been queuing with the Snobbish Hobo earlier on at the Civic Centre. He had jaywalked from the other side of the road to accost his white friend.

'Hau! I thought he was your friend,' exclaimed Theks. 'Anyway, it doesn't matter where he stands to ask for some help.'

'Are you giving preference to this man who has been exploiting us all at the expense of those who have been fighting for your rights?' asked the man, wagging his forefinger at Theks. 'Can't you see that this shit has played with his chance; he left his job at Transnet of his own accord. I have never even had the chance of being employed. That's why I became an MK soldier, to fight for you and me. Fighting so that you could get a chance of better education,' said the homeless man, looking at the books we were carrying. 'Are you now telling me that our sacrifices are worth nothing?'

Theks was left speechless. I decided to give the man a five rand coin in an attempt to calm him down. The coin did the trick and the two hobos' differences were resolved.

The pavement was clogged with street vendors. People were moving along in a hurry. It was even difficult for the two of us to walk side by side. Theks chose to remain silent as she mulled over the words of the homeless man who had challenged her kindness.

As we negotiated our way alongside a stall, trying to push through the viscous traffic on the pavement, Theks suddenly stopped and picked up a small running shoe.

'Wow! Thembi has asked me to buy her some takkies for her birthday,' she said, examining the running shoe. 'You know winter is coming and if I don't buy her a pair now they'll be expensive.' She held the running shoe up. 'What do you think? Beautiful, né?'

I took the running shoe and examined it.

'Hau! Cheap as well, né.'

'Only eighty rand Mama,' interrupted the black vendor. His pronunciation of 'eighty' sounded like 'eti'.

'Serious?' asked Theks.

'Sure Mama. Me give Mama discount eighty rand,' said the seller.

'I think I should get it for Thembi.'

'Why not? A Nike shoe for eighty rand is a bargain.'

'What size do you want, Mama?' asked the vendor as if Theks had already decided on buying the shoe.

As Theks was thinking, I examined the shoe. It was different from other Nike shoes I knew. The logo on this particular shoe pointed in the opposite direction. Suspiciously I looked again: the logo started with a letter M instead of the usual N. Because of our over-familiarity with the Nike logo, we had nearly bought a fake product. We were about to buy a Mike shoe.

'Yerrrr! Don't. It's a fong-kong,' I warned Theks under my breath.

'What? You lie?'

She snatched the shoe from my hand to examine it.

'Look! It's Mike not Nike. It's not the real McCoy.'

'That is size four, Mama. Me can give you all size on discount, Mama,' said the vendor.

Theks finished examining the fake Nike shoe and put it down with a feigned smile. She picked up another one with the label Reobuk. The amusement induced by the fake brands had made her forget about the words of the hobo. Adding to our amusement was the fact that each time we picked up an item the vendor would call out the price. He would immediately promise us discounts that we never even asked for.

'Eeei-sh! What time are you leaving this place?' Theks asked, trying to rescue us. 'You know I don't have enough money in my purse.'

'Fife, Mama,' replied the seller while raising five fingers. 'Can I put this away for you when you come back?'

'Iyaa. Can you?' she asked doubtfully.

'Yes, Mama.'

'That will be great. Thank you very much.'

'What time you is back, Mama?'

'Forty minutes or so. I'm just going to that FNB bank,' she said, glancing at her wristwatch.

'OK, Mama. Me wait for you.'

We negotiated our way through the crowded stalls on the pavement. We were no longer interested in buying anything. We were too busy trying to figure out whether everything sold by those vendors was a fake.

ten

It was busy in the Jo'burg city centre. Everybody was trying to make money. We crossed Commissioner Street to get to the taxi rank next to the Carlton Centre. The taxi queue marshals were busy calling loudly in Zulu.

'Orlando, Dube, Phefeni lapha side. Chiawelo, Mapetla, Protea this side. Naledi, Zola, Mndeni wozani ngapha.' Each one of them pointed at the minibus-taxis that were standing there.

'Hey wena msunukanyoko ng'the ugibele kuleya taxi ebomvu 'mangabe uya eProtea hay' kulena maan. Hey you, your mother's cunt! I said board the red taxi if you are going to Protea and not this one,' shouted one of the queue marshals. He was abusing a male commuter in a blue suit and tie who had mistakenly boarded the wrong taxi.

'Manj' ung' thukelani, pho? But why insult me like that?' asked the shocked commuter.

While pointing at his right ear, the taxi queue marshal answered. 'Angith' awuzwa la emandhleben' wakho. Because you are deaf.'

'Ingan' ngiya kuzwa manje. But I am hearing you now.'

The queue marshal began to roll up the sleeves of his blue shirt as if in preparation for a fight. 'Ufunukulwa masimbakho? Do you want to fight, you shitpot?'

A second queue marshal came and asked with indignation in his voice: 'Wuthin' lowomdlwembe? What is that stray dog saying?'

'Lenja yicabanga ukuthi yihlakaniphe ukundlula wonke umuntu olana. This dog thinks he is cleverer than everybody else,' answered the first queue marshal in an angry voice.

'Nisamelen? Hini ning'shayi lowomgodoyi? Niyawusaba hini? What are you still waiting for? Why don't you just beat that stray dog? Are you afraid of it?' shouted another minibus-taxi driver, showing his solidarity with the first queue marshal.

The driver got out of the minibus. The engine was still running, but he didn't apologise to the commuters who were seated inside waiting to leave. In his right hand he was carrying a sledgehammer. As he approached, an elderly woman pleaded with him.

'Kodwa bantwa' bam' lomfana angezanga lutho ukuthi nimshaye. But my children, this boy has done nothing to deserve your beatings.'

'Thula wenasfebe-salukazi ndunu-ndalandini angikhulumi nawe. Shut up you old prostitute bitch because I'm not talking to you,' snapped the queue marshal.

'Unga khulumi namikanjalo, angiyona intangayakho. Abakufundisanga ekhaya uma usakhula ukuthi umuntu omdala uyahlonitswa? Don't talk to me like that because I'm not of the same age as you. Didn't they teach you at your home how to respect your elders?' protested the senior citizen.

'Or uzongenzani uma ngingakuhloniphi? Uzonginyobisa? Se uqhanyelwe hini salukazindini? Or what are you going to do if I don't respect you? Will you fuck me? Are you feeling randy you old woman?' replied the queue marshal haughtily.

'Shoo! Imhlola ayiphelibakithi! Wazewang'thuka lomuntu. Kodwa Unkulunkulu makakubusise. Shoo! Miracles never cease! This person has insulted me. But may God bless you,' said the old lady, trying to remain strong. But her face revealed that the insults had upset her.

'Madoda yekelan' ukuphikisana nalezompatha siqhubeke ngomsebezi. Abelungu balindile. Gentlemen, stop competing with those fools and let's continue with the job. People are waiting,' shouted another taxi-driver.

The smart commuter who had been insulted had kept quiet, but it was evident that the insults that had been unleashed on the old woman, who had been trying to protect him, had angered him. I looked at the senior citizen; she was busy dabbing the corners of her eyes with her handkerchief. Theks glared at the queue marshal.

'Voetsek ung' bekeni wena? Or uyangifensa hini? Fuck you, why are you looking at me? Or do you fancy me?' swore the queue marshal.

'Leave those idiots alone,' I whispered to Theks.

'Basop! Ngeliny' langa uzonya mfanam' uma ungijwayela kabi. Be careful. One day you will shit, my son, if you undermine me again,' warned the queue marshal, wagging his finger at the smart commuter.

We all followed the instructions of the queue marshal as he ushered us into the waiting minibus-taxis. He was spitting all sorts of insults at any commuters he thought were disobeying his orders. When the commuters justifiably complained about being crammed into worn-out seats, they were told to 'fuck off'. If they complained to the driver about the speed at which the taxi was travelling, they were threatened with being thrown out of the taxi before their journey was complete. When they complained about loud music played by the insensitive driver, they were accused of being jealous. We were all aware that the drivers were capable of stopping the taxi at any time and whipping a passenger with the sjamboks that they always carry with them. The likelihood is that other drivers would also join in the assault without even bothering to ask the reason. If you dare to throw a punch in self-defence you might well end up being killed. The best thing to do is to remain calm and pray that you arrive home safely.

I had learnt this the hard way after trying to reason with a taxi driver as I was returning home to Orlando West from Chiawelo in Soweto after visiting my mother. At about half-past eight in the evening on the Old Potchefstroom road I stopped a Bara-bound taxi. It was nearly full of commuters. Along the way I gave the driver a twenty rand banknote, expecting him to give me eighteen rand and fifty cents change. After driving a few kilometres without getting my change, I decided to remind him. The taxi driver denied that I had given him any money. We had a heated argument. I had several witnesses inside the taxi who had seen me giving him the money, but he denied everything until we reached Bara. He then called some of his friends and told them that I was trying to take an advantage of him by having a free ride. I was instructed to stay inside the taxi whilst the frightened commuters who sympathised with me were forced to get out.

Once all the commuters had disembarked the taxi made a U-turn, with me kidnapped inside. I was being held tightly by two muscular guys who began showering me with all sorts of insults and telling me all the bad things they would do to me. I knew I had done nothing wrong; they were the ones who should have been apologising to me. I tried to stay calm, not knowing what to do.

As we passed the Klipspruit-Pimville railway bridge we saw a group of people walking. My three captors began to debate whether to pick the commuters up. As they stopped to let the people get into the taxi, they instructed me to stay where I was while they opened the door. They ushered the commuters into the back seat, leaving me to sit on my own immediately behind the driver with a female passenger who was carrying some groceries in plastic bags.

Before the taxi could move forward, the lady asked me if she could sit by the window where I was; she wanted to be able to balance her groceries against it. I looked at my two captors who nodded their approval. As we exchanged seats I saw that one person was still standing outside, waiting to get into the taxi. Since the door was open I jumped outside and ran for my life.

I ran through the squatter camp in the direction of Kliptown, with my captors pursuing me as if I was their most wanted quarry. Everywhere dogs were barking and the inhabitants of the squatter camp were peeping around their doors. Some were helping my pursuers to locate me. Some were whistling loudly, enjoying the spectacle as I ran for my life. Some even splashed me with dirty water.

I ran out of the squatter camp and towards the nearby cemetery. The distant barking of the dogs and the fading footsteps suggested to me that I had outrun my captors, but they hadn't given up the chase.

Then, because of the darkness of the night and the moonless horizon, I bumped against a gravestone in the cemetery. I felt a pain in my shin and warm blood oozing down my leg. Seconds later I could not run any more. I fell on top of the concrete level of one of the graves with my head against the epitaph.

As I lay on the grave trying to breathe quietly, I heard footsteps coming closer as my pursuers searched for me. Next to the ghostly bluegum trees I heard two gunshots fired into the air, but I didn't move from my hiding-place. I tried to breathe quietly, hoping my pursuers wouldn't be able to locate me in the darkness.

Eventually the footsteps withdrew and two further gunshots were fired. I started panting hard with terror as they retreated, but remained lying on the grave until I was convinced that they had gone. I did this even though the fear of the dead was starting to gnaw at my mind.

That night I had to limp home via the then notorious Nancefield Hostel. I wouldn't risk hitchhiking for fear that I would be picked up by my kidnappers. The pain that I had the following day was indescribable, but I never told anybody what had actually happened.

eleven

Theks and myself remained seated uncomfortably on the back seat of the noisy death-trap minibus. It ran hell for leather along Commissioner Street via John Vorster Square. Ear-splitting music was blasting from a pair of speakers right behind us. The bass was pounding my eardrums, but the driver and the two teenagers in front of us were nodding along to Joe Nina.

> Maria Podesta maan. Ding-dong.
> Yeah, yeah, yeah baby.
> Ungishaya ding, ding ding ding-dong.

It was so loud that it was difficult for people sitting next to each other to have any kind of conversation. To see if it was time for us to pay for the taxi fare we had to concentrate on the gestures of the people in front of us as they started counting their money.

In front of me a black plastic refuse bag had been sellotaped across a broken window. As the minibus trundled away from the green light of the robot the plastic started making a rankling noise. Just next to the refuse bag was a sticker:

I LIKE YOUR PERM, BUT NOT ON MY WINDOW

Before I could point that out to Theks, I leaned backward, trying to stifle my amusement. But that amusement was short-lived as I was pricked by the sharp metal edge of the worn-out leatherette seat.

The old minibus skidded at the red robots along Main Reef

Road near the Fordsburg Shopping Mall. I watched Theks as she shut her eyes with fright. The minibus started to yaw all over the road. There were screams from the commuters inside. Fortunately, the driver managed to control the skid by applying the brakes just before he collided with the BP petrol tanker that had come to a halt in front of us. Most of us had already covered our faces with our hands, praying silently. When our short prayers were answered with that near miss, I began to feel trapped; I couldn't adjust my cramped legs and my knees were almost touching my chin.

The robot changed to green, but before the driver could accelerate away the passenger door, which was fastened by a wire, swung open. The guy sitting next to it was instructed to hold onto the door until the driver was able to pull the taxi onto the side of the road. Since the indicator and brake lights of his minibus were dead, the driver waved his hand out of his window to signal to the other road users that he intended to move his car into the slower lane. A white 3-series BMW Dolphin came speeding up from behind. Its driver was forced to make an emergency stop, the tires screeching on the road to avoid an accident. In a sudden flash the two drivers were swearing at each other.

'Where did you buy your driver's licence, you moron? Don't you know to indicate when you have to change lanes? You think this is your road?' shouted the white bearded man inside the BMW.

'I bought it from your mother's arse,' retorted the minibus driver.

'Your mind is as short as your hair, you piece of shit.'

'Go fuck yourself, you white bastard.'

'Who do you think you are? You think democracy means running around driving the way you like without thinking? You uncivilised black shit!'

'You can suck my dick. I don't give a shit about you, you racist bastard.'

'Neither your skorokoro taxi nor your kaffir dick can even buy a mirror on this car. I wonder if you have insurance or if you even know what the word means.'

'Insurance is your bitch mother's wrinkled pussy.'

The BMW driver clicked his tongue to express his anger.

'People don't know how to talk in this city. All they do is shout and swear at each other,' said Theks.

I craned my neck above everyone in order to see what was going on. I glimpsed the static speedo as well as another two stickers attached to the back of the driver's seat. They read:

**JUST BECAUSE YOU KNOW ME
DOES NOT MEAN YOU DO NOT
HAVE TO PAY ME.**

And:

**NEVER ARGUE WITH A FOOL, PEOPLE
MIGHT NOT NOTICE THE DIFFERENCE**

The BMW pulled away as the minibus driver stopped on the side of the road to fasten the passenger door with the wire. Outside I could see several people busy hammering tin and timber together. They were making shelters for themselves on open ground not far from the road. Two women were standing next to a newly completed shack, one of them dandling a bare-chested baby.

The previous week when I passed by in a taxi on my way home the place was just open ground, but since then the shanty houses had mushroomed. They had covered almost the whole area through what they call 'affirmative occupation'.

Everything is 'affirmative' nowadays, I thought to myself. Slums or squatter camps have become 'affirmative settlements'. Shoplifting is called 'affirmative transaction'. Carjackers make 'affirmative repossessions'. Even going out with a white person is an 'affirmative romance'.

The driver of the minibus taxi returned to his seat. He scratched his head and swore under his breath. He had just realised that he had unwittingly stalled the engine when he went to fasten the door, forgetting that it didn't have a starter motor.

'Give me a push,' said the driver to the two boys next to him as he slumped into the seat. 'This car won't start.'

The two boys got out. I followed them to stretch my aching legs.

'Just a sec,' said the driver.

He bowed his head next to the pedals and bit on the red wire next to the ignition, then connected it to another red wire. The driver looked at the temperature gauge; it was the only thing that worked on his dashboard. The minibus was overheating. Just above the temperature gauge there were two red flickering lights, one of which lit up a red battery sign to show that there was a misconnection somewhere. Without even apologising to his commuters for the delay, the driver got out of the taxi, lifted his seat and looked at the engine. Not knowing where to start, he touched the coil. 'Eish,' he cried, as he felt the heat burn the tips of his fingers.

'Shit! It must be the connection here. The points are not open enough. That bastard! I told him,' said the driver to himself. 'Please get me a number eight there in the cabin,' he said to me.

I ran to the other side of the taxi and searched the glove box. It was full of spanners and screwdrivers. I came back with a small spanner with the number eight stamped on its head and gave it to him. Without a word of thanks he started to undo the bolts on the air filter. Not having a clue of what he was doing, the driver shook the carburettor before unhooking the black tubes that connect the distributor to it. He took two screwdrivers and opened the jet on the carburettor with both of them. After being satisfied with his job he fastened it back. He then opened the distributor and unhooked the condenser. With some rough paper on the dashboard he started cleaning the condenser and the distributor. The driver examined the condenser briefly and then reconnected it to the distributor and began exchanging the wires from the transistor to the coil. I looked inside the engine. There was no fan belt to cool it, but at the bottom of the engine I caught a glimpse of some oil-grimed pantyhose, which had snapped.

'Your fan belt is broken,' I told him.

'OK, that could be the reason,' said the driver, fishing the broken pantyhose out of the engine. He tied them together again before putting them back in place of the fan belt.

All the commuters were out of the minibus by that stage. Water was running out of the leaking radiator and black oil was forming a pool on the road. One man was busy urinating on the pavement not very far away from where the others were standing. By and by the driver finished what he was doing and leapt inside. The commuters followed, except for the two teenagers, the guy who was urinating on the pavement and myself. After he had turned the ignition with his screwdriver, the taxi driver shouted to the passengers to 'push!' We pushed for a few metres then all of a sudden the engine started to roar. He smiled as we got inside again.

The taxi moved along slowly in first gear. Theks started smiling; she was looking at the squatter camp by the side of the road. I smiled back at her.

'What name will be given to this affirmative settlement?' she asked curiously.

'Well. Let me see,' I said mulling it over, 'there are lots of Mandela Views already. Maybe Mbekiville?'

'Whaa! I don't think so because we already have one next to Fourways,' said Theks.

'No! That one is called Diepsloot.'

'No, it's not,' she insisted.

'OK then. How about Sisuluville.'

'Or Sobukwetown.'

'Modiseville.'

People use the names of famous political leaders to attract the

81

government's attention to the urgent need for housing. It is also a clever tactic to delay any possible eviction that might follow.

Next to the main road I saw children playing hide and seek. They ran into the dumpsite between the shacks. One child wearing a tattered blue T-shirt hid behind a tin shack with NO 3814 painted on the outside. A thin black dog followed him. The dog started pissing on the grass nearby.

'I wonder if that address is recognised for postal delivery?' asked Theks.

twelve

Half a dozen of ngudus (quarts of beer) stood in front of us. Dunga, Themba, Vusi and myself were sitting outside my home on Vilakazi Street in Orlando West. There was no one at home and I guessed that they were still trying to vote at the nearest polling station.

My brother's hi-fi speakers were pumping out some fat kwaito beats outside on the lawn.

Hini lethi ncancanca lomshini wuyakhuluma.	(What is saying ncancanca? This machine is talking.)
Wamnandi ubeer. Ngabebawukhanda ngani?	(Beer is tasty. I wonder how they make it?)
Histokvel.	(It's a stokvel.)
Hay' mina! Ngoyofeletswaleni kwenzenjani.	(Oh me! I am going to die in the beer place.)

Themba sang along with Woza Africa's *iStokvel* . Meanwhile Vusi was busy talking. He was eight years older than I was and a former MK cadre. I only knew him through Themba and I didn't like him much. He was now working for the new National Defence Force.

He was boasting about his skill stripping and reassembling guns. He carried two pistols with him, which were to be used during that night in a gunfire salute to the birth of democracy. Vusi had given me the unlicensed one to hold while stripping the other one. There were no bullets in the one that I was holding. According to his story, he had taken that pistol from some guys while doing roadblock duty on the Soweto Highway.

As an MK cadre, Vusi had fought as a guerrilla against the apartheid government from a base in Lusaka. He had told us of his involvement in acts of sabotage against apartheid structures. We had listened to him like a group of kindergarten kids; he made us feel that those of us who didn't go into exile never actually fought against apartheid.

I was still holding Vusi's unlicensed pistol when two beautiful girls passed by. Themba stopped singing and wolf-whistled them. The ladies looked back in our direction and Themba stuck out his tongue in a juvenile tease. The ladies reduced their gait. He slid his tongue around his lips and curled it around the corners of his mouth. The ladies threw back inviting smiles.

'Wow! The blacker the berry, the sweeter the juice,' I muttered.

With his drunken gaze still following the ladies, Themba continued. 'The darker the skin, the deeper the roots.'

'When have you guys become interested in kids? Com' on gents, those chicks are still very young,' cautioned Dunga. 'I am sure their mothers still wash their panties for them. I don't even think they undergo ladies circle yet.'

'Never!' said Themba. 'Just look at their breasts, man! Kids don't have that kind of dairy. They could feed the whole of Soweto.'

'Sure. You're playing. Those chicks can show you a real game, man,' added Vusi, pointing at Dunga with his forefinger. 'Don't underestimate them; they have sugar daddies and big holes.'

'Ag shit, man! If they can be horny then they are ready, man,' I said. 'Why bother? Fuck the age of consent anyway. It is against the act of nature.'

'Yeah, we might even find that they are already mothers with two or three kids,' added Themba.

'Oh shit! Look at that ATM, man!' said Vusi, referring to the girls' buttocks. 'That's a real African Trade Mark. Just go try your luck, guys.'

'But guys, come on. We're still enjoying ourselves here,' said Dunga.

'Joe, don't be selfish,' I pleaded with him. 'You can dance between Theks' legs anytime to celebrate this big day and we don't have chicks, man. Let us also enjoy.'

'OK. Go on. But be careful.'

'Of what?'

'Z3.'

'I don't think those chicks have AIDS, man. They are still new in the game,' I said.

'Don't be surprised if you get electrocuted, my bra.'

'And we'll be there to take you to your RDP house at Avalon cemetery,' added Vusi.

Themba and I caught up with the two ladies and asked if we could join them. Themba had walked ahead of me and hooked up with the one that I had eyes for. Within a short space of time he was already busy with his flirtatious talk. I had to keep up the standard that he had already set by making the other lady giggle. I summoned up my courage and managed to say some words as we flopped down Vilakazi Street.

'Hi, sweetheart.'

With a very cold voice she answered. 'I'm not your sweetheart.'

'I know,' I said, intoxicated with humiliation.

'So why do you sweetheart me if you know?' she asked with her attention fixed on her friend in front of us.

'Because I know you'll be my sweetheart soon.'

'What makes you think that?' she barked.

'Because today should be a special day for everyone, and everyone should have a special someone to share this day with.'

'Not me.'

The lady was not impressed with me. Before I could respond, Themba's companion was giggling at his attempts at flattery.

'You sound unhappy,' I tried again. 'Has somebody troubled you?'

'No.'

I was running out of ideas. I didn't know how to withdraw. I looked at her hair. It was shiny and had been carefully relaxed with curling tongs. 'Will you accept a compliment?' I asked.

'That depends on whether it is a good compliment.'

'And if is a bad one what will you do?'

'I always get emotional and insult the person.'

'Whose lips would you use to insult me? I don't think your beautiful ones could do such a thing,' I gushed.

For the first time she chuckled and revealed her dimples. I had initially thought that she was less attractive than her friend, but when she smiled and exposed her dimples I instantly changed my mind.

'You never know. Just try it,' she said.

'Are you sure that you are ready to hear an honest compliment?'

'Are you ready to stomach the result?'

Her friend, who was walking with Themba, looked back at us. I looked at my companion; it seemed to me that the reason she didn't want to speak to me was because I looked like a typical township tsotsi in my no-name blue jeans that had seen better days and my All Star takkies.

My companion was wearing fashionable pink-striped trainers, a pink miniskirt and T-shirt. My breath smelled of alcohol while she smelled of expensive perfume. From the curtness in her talk I knew that she had initially wished me away, but I didn't want to spoil Themba's chances.

'Yes, I think so. I'm ready to stomach the result,' I said, unsure of what to expect.

'So go on.'

'Well, actually my main reason for coming over to talk to you was to tell you how elegant your hairstyle looks this evening.'

'You lie!' she said coyly, pressing her hair very lightly with her right hand.

'Honestly.'

'It's too early to assess beauty on this street,' she replied, looking at me. 'Just wait until later and you'll see for yourself.'

'So is that the reason you have decided to look immaculate?'

Before she could answer that question Themba, who was swaggering like a bridegroom, looked back at us and smiled. He was good at winning the girls. I noticed his arm around the girl's waist as they strolled along. I stealthily tried to seize my compion's waist, but as I did so I felt Vusi's pistol in my waistband. I momentarily pulled my face. I didn't like guns. I had thought that he had taken it from me earlier on. As I was wondering what to do Neo, Theks' brother, passed us on his way home from his car wash business by the shops.

'Joe, there is no sexual harassment here in the township, man,' teased Neo as he passed us. 'Just put your arm around her like Themba.'

A wave of embarrassment crept inside me. I attempted to smile at Neo, but the smile failed to come to my lips. What he suggested was my exact feeling. I wanted to hold my companion, but didn't have the guts.

'Actually, tomorrow is my birthday,' the lady delivered me from my embarrassment.

'I wish I knew you before so that I could be invited to your big day.'

'It's just a small party.'

'Then how are you going to deal with gatecrashers like myself?'

'I'll chase them away,' she said smiling.

'Even if you know me?'

'I don't know you.'

I immediately remembered that I had forgotten to introduce myself to the lady.

'I was actually saving my introduction for last, but I'm glad you brought it up.'

'Is that so?' she asked, not convinced by my lie.

'Yeah. So tell me, do you have a name? Because if you don't, or if I feel it doesn't suit you, I would like to give you a new one.'

'I'm Nkanyezi.'

'I'm Dingz. Nice to meet you Nkanyezi, you are indeed a star as your name suggests; there is no reason to give you a new name because you have the perfect one.'

'Thank you.'

'I would have called you Sunshine if I felt that your name didn't fit.'

There was a pause as she smiled broadly.

'So where do you live, Nkanyezi?'

'Here in Dube opposite the shops. That house with a blue wall.'

We were passing the house where the street party was going to happen. There were a few people putting up a big tent in the backyard. I could also hear kwaito music coming from the open door of the house. One of the guys who were helping with the tent greeted Nkanyezi. They then exchanged some jokes about that night's party. Another guy was busy talking to Themba's companion. We waited briefly on the pavement. Two cars facing in opposite directions were parked right in the middle of the street. The two drivers were busy exchanging some worldly jokes at the top of their voices. A red microbus came from behind us, but the two drivers didn't bother to move. Instead the microbus driver had to share the small pavement with us in order to negotiate his way through. We were forced to walk in single file along the pavement so that the microbus could pass. The pavement had just been sprayed with water to wash away the dust in preparation for the party and there was still some water in the little pot-holes. Themba paddled through a pothole that he hadn't seen as he attempted to flinch away from the microbus.

'Oh shit!' he swore at his misfortune.

The microbus driver then drove through another pothole and splashed all of us with dirty water. To add to Themba's woes, he was hit on the shoulder by the wing mirror of the microbus.

'Ag! Fuckshit!' he screamed.

I looked at Themba whose cream jeans were soaked with dirty

water and tried to hold back my laughter. Meanwhile the driver of the microbus had stopped a few metres ahead of us.

'What are they waiting for?' asked Nkanyezi.

'I don't know. Maybe it's some of our friends who have recognised us.'

'I see,' she said, unconvinced.

As soon as we approached the microbus, the driver, who seemed to have had one too many, beckoned to us. Themba and myself said goodbye to the ladies, pretending that we knew the guys.

'Enjoy your birthday tomorrow,' I said to Nkanyezi.

'Thanks. I will,' she replied, as the two of them turned the corner and disappeared.

Themba and myself went over to the driver's window. There were two other men inside; the passenger sitting next to the driver had a scarred face, and the man sitting behind them had a thick cupid's bow (a thick upper lip and a thin lower lip).

'Benizama ukujabulisa I'febezenu ngathi? Were you trying to impress your bitches through us?' barked the driver.

'Ngani manje? Why?' asked Themba, bewildered.

'Musukuzibayizisa ngoba niyazi ngiring'a ngani. Don't try to pretend you don't know what I am talking about, because you know exactly what I mean.'

'Angazi mina. Or uyacava wena, braDingz? I don't know, do you have any idea, bra Dingz?' asked Themba, looking at me.

'Eintlik udenka ukuthi uslim, né? You think you are clever, né?' asked the indignant driver.

'Joe. Angicavi ukuthi uring'a ngani? Man, I don't know what you are talking about?'

'OK, kleva. Benishokubani ukuthifuckshit? To whom were you saying fuckshit?'

'No. Besingabekisanga kini. We weren't directing it at you.'

'Benishokubani manje? Where were you directing it?'

'Ngibeng' zikhulumela nje ngingashokumuntu. I was just talking haphazardly without referring to any person.'

'Uyahlanya hini noma ucabanga ukuthi minangiyahlanya? Are you mad or do you think I'm mad?' fumed the driver, wriggling his forefinger next to his right ear.

'Mina angihlanyi. Angaziwena. I'm not mad. I don't know about you,' snapped Themba.

'Uphinda ubenenkani msunuwakho. You have to have guts to be arrogant, you arsehole.'

Suddenly a burgundy Toyota Sprinter that was going in the opposite direction hooted at the microbus. The driver of the Toyota Sprinter waved to the microbus driver and flashed the headlights. He stopped right in the middle of the road and the two drivers began to talk.

'Wola kawu. Hi, my friend,' shouted the driver of the Toyota Sprinter to the microbus driver.

'Wola.'

'Zishaphi vandag? Where is the gig today?'

'Ziyawa kahijampas. Its happening here in the evening.'

'Khona kahi? Around here?'

'Yebo,' confirmed the microbus driver.

'Uzozwakala nawesbali? Will you also come?'

'Ngizobona. Ngisahlanganisa amasente. I'll see. I'm still trying to get a few cents together,' answered the microbus driver.

'Manje awufake umzamolapho. Please give me the stuff,' said the driver of the Sprinter, rubbing both his palms together; a gesture that I could only guess referred to dagga.

'Kuntswembu sbali. Mhlawumbe jampas. It's bad sbali. Maybe in the evening.'

'Manje amajita akho nawo vele? So your guys don't have as well?'

'Kublind. They don't.'

'Eintlik lababoytwo angibacavi. Ngabobani? Anyway I don't know those two. Who are they?' enquired the driver of the Toyota Sprinter.

'Nami angizicavi lezinja. Zisikhonkote ngenhlamba la erhawundini. Manje siyozifundisa abantu. I don't know these dogs either. They insulted us along the way. So we are going to teach them.' I could see what was coming and felt obliged to apologise to the driver before there was a fight.

'Siyaxolisa umangabe uyithathe kanjalogrootman. We apologise if you took it that way, brother.'

'Hey! Akuxoliswa ngaleyondlela. Or ubona uJesu la? Hey! That is not the way to apologise, or do you see Jesus here?' growled the guy with the thick cupid's bow, who was chewing gum.

'Nixolisa ngani? Niphethe malinilapho? What are you apologising with? How much do you have with you?' asked the scarfaced passenger.

'Asinamali. Sisafunda. We have no money. We are students,' I replied.

'Kodwa hini kufanele sixolise singezanga lutho? But why should we be remorseful for something we did not do?' protested Themba.

'Wena engathinguwe unenkani? It seems you are the one who is arrogant,' said the driver taking out a small silver gun.

'Kodwa . . . But . . .'

'Kodwakodwaini? But-but what?'

'Lethani amawallets wenu la. Give me your wallets,' ordered scarface.

With my cold sweating hand I hesitantly gave my wallet to scarface. It contained my last fifty rand. Themba, who had nerves of steel, refused to hand his over. The driver took the money from inside and threw my wallet back at me.

'Now fuck off!' said the driver of the microbus, revving the engine.

I watched helplessly as the microbus sped off down the street. The Toyota Sprinter made a U-turn and followed it in the direction of the main road to Mofolo North. As they drove away a sticker next to the brake lights caught my eye. It was written in bold black lettering:

THOUGH I DRIVE IN THE VALLEY OF THE SHADOW OF DEATH I FEAR NO HIJACKERS, BUT ANOTHER FUEL INCREASE

thirteen

Dunga and Vusi were still sitting on the lawn outside my house drinking beer. Theks and Lerato, Theks's friend who lived a few blocks away, had joined them. It was obvious that Lerato had been organised to accompany Vusi to the street party. Loud kwaito music that was coming from the house of the street party organisers overpowered the music we were playing. A pleasing smell of braaied meat also permeated the air.

Themba and I had agreed not to say anything about the guys in the microbus. I was embarrassed at my lack of courage and didn't want them to know that I had been robbed so easily.

As we arrived Dunga started giving us a tongue-lashing. 'You guys are useless. What took you so long? What were you doing with those kids?'

'Chatting up ladies is not an easy job, my bra,' answered Themba.

'Suka! Don't pretend as if you are mafikizolo in the game. You have fathered three kids by different ladies,' snapped Dunga.

'What if I tell you that the mothers of my kids were of easy virtue?'

'How could you talk of Nthabi like that?' interrupted Theks.

'Because we have fallen apart,' replied Themba.

'Since when have you stopped being so possessive?' asked Vusi.

'Since we fell apart last week.'

'Speak of the devil, here she comes now,' I lied playfully.

'Where?' asked Themba looking around in every direction.

'Just kidding. I wanted to see if you were telling the truth.'

'Of course not. She's still mine.'

'So where is my gun?' asked Vusi in a worried voice.

'I lost it,' I replied.

'What? Voetsek wena! Don't shit on my head please,' said Vusi. 'Give me the gun before I lose my temper. Because if I lose my temper I will make you find it with only one bullet from this other one.'

'It's true. We've lost the gun,' confirmed Themba. 'And the reason we came back late is that we were still searching for it.'

'I hope you have not bartered it for sexual favours,' said Dunga, nosing at my pants like a dog.

'You lie. There it is,' said Vusi with a relieved voice when he saw the bulge in my waistband.

I went inside the house to see my aunt who had been away when we arrived earlier during the day. I found her seated on the sofa with two female Jehovah's Witnesses. They were trying to convince her to convert to their church.

My aunt had not been near the church recently. I knew this was due to one of the preachers, as I had overheard her relating the story to my uncle the other day. According to her account it all happened during one of those never-ending collections. The collection had begun with donations of ten rand, but because my aunt didn't have a ten rand banknote, she had donated her last five rand coin.

After the collection the preacher had stood in the pulpit and told the congregation that there were still some people around them who took the church for granted, and used her five rand coin as an example. Since that day she preferred to go to church only when she had enough money. This meant that, as a pensioner, she had to wait until her monthly allowance came in before she could set foot in church. I felt sorry for my aunt. She had been a servant of that church for almost half of a century.

'Oh Dingz, I nearly forgot. Your brother left some money for you to pay for the electricity and rent at the municipality office,' said my aunt. 'That is, if you will have the time?'

I hesitated; I could suddenly see a way out of my cashless situation; I could use the rent money to celebrate the elections and then get Dunga to bail me out when he got paid at month-end.

'I think I will,' I stammered. 'Because my first class is at eleven. But I'm not sure whether I will be able to come straight home tomorrow,' I said doubtfully.

'Well, you can bring the receipts on Friday then when you come home. You will come home, won't you?'

'Yes, of course I will,' I replied.

'OK then, just look under my pillow and you'll see one hundred and eighty rand.'

I went into her room and found the money. Instead of putting it somewhere safe I put it in my pocket. Then I went to the kitchen and grabbed the last three ngudus from the refrigerator. I sidled out carrying the bottles – to the disgust of my aunt, who shook her grey head with disapproval.

As I came out of the house I found two guys standing with my friends on the lawn. They were carrying a big travelling bag with some stolen goods inside. Themba looked very interested in the items: a Rotel amplifier, a Sony video recorder and a Sansui CD player. He was trying to strike a good bargain with the two guys, who sounded desperately in need of cash. I put the beers down on the lawn and opened one with my teeth.

'Manje nizibayisamalini lezinto? So how much are you selling these goods for?' asked Themba in his tsotsitaal township lingo.

'Eintlik isound yivaya threeklipa. Ivideo singakugaya ngeklipa. In fact the music is three hundred rand. But we can give you the video at hundred rand,' said one of the guys, pointing at the goods.

'Eintlik nizivusaphi lezinto? Where did you actually get these things from?' asked Dunga, concern in his voice.

'Eintlik sigaywezona henye ingamla ebesiyispanela kada emakhishini. In fact a white man we have been working for in the suburb gave them to us,' replied the other guy.

'Niyajiya nizibathulile lezinto madoda. You lie, you have stolen these goods, gentleman,' I said.

'Asijiyi grootmaan. Ingamla yakhona beyithuthela eStates beseyisinikeza lezinto. We are not telling lies, brother. That white man in question was emigrating to the States and he gave us these things.'

'Beniyitshunela ini? What were you doing for him?' asked Dunga.

'Besiyipendela idladla ukuthiyizolibayisa kada eSandton. We were painting his house for him so that he could sell it there at Sandton.'

'Athini amanumbers wakhe sim'belele manje? What are his numbers so that we can call him now?'

'Akasigayanga. He didn't give them to us.'

'Sibize amagaata azoconfirma? Can we call the police to confirm?' snapped Vusi.

'Ningayitshuni leyo, magents. Eintlik siziphandile lezinto. Please don't, gentleman. It's true we have stolen these things.'

'Nizithola va? Where do you get them?' asked Vusi.

'Sitabalaze khona kada emakhishini. We stole them there at the suburb.'

'Manjenifuna ukuthisibaye nizophinda nisispinele zona vele? So you want us to buy them so that you can come and steal them from us again?' asked Themba.

'Angeke groot, siyakuthembisa. We wont, brother, we promise you.'

Themba took out his wallet and opened it. I looked enviously at the money inside. 'OK. Mina ngiphethe itwo klipa but ngizifuna zonke. OK, I only have two hundred but I want them all,' he said.

'Manje awusafaki nomahi fivetiger nyana grootmaan? Uzoba ungalahlanga. But brother, please add just fifty rand. You wouldn't have lost much,' pleaded the guy.

'OK. Ngizofaka itwotiger kuphela. OK. I will add twenty rand only.'

'Iya, imoja nayo. Yes, that is also fine.'

'Manje iyasebenza ledulas? So are these stolen goods working?' asked Themba.

'Imoja kakhula. Or ufuna sikuthestele yona before sivaya? It's perfect. Or do you want us to test it for you before we go?'

'Nisure? Are you sure?'

'Asigadli. We are not lying.'

'OK. Bambani la. OK. Take here,' said Themba giving one of the guys two hundred and twenty rand in banknotes.

'Ncanda nantsi, nebonsela. Here they are, as well as your free gift,' said one of the guys, handing over the stolen goods as well as three jazz CDs: Keith Jarrett's *Nude Ants*, Miles Davis's *Live* and Julian Joseph's *Reality*.

After the two guys had left, Dunga started arguing with Themba about buying stolen goods.

'Those goods might have been stolen from your relative or even from your own home, do you know that?' chided Dunga angrily.

'Since when have you become a saint?' replied Themba. 'Have you forgotten that you bought the speakers for your music system from the same people?'

'That was two years ago.'

'It doesn't matter when it was. You must start by blaming the man in the mirror before you blame me for committing the same act, my friend,' said Themba.

I never uttered a word, but in a way I sided with Dunga.

After checking the stolen goods for damage, Themba asked me to take them inside the house for the time being until he was ready to take them home with him.

fourteen

The sound of trains slowing up at nearby Phefeni station echoed through the neighbourhood. It was growing dark outside. The music was getting louder and there were the sounds of revving cars and shouting in the street. It was easy to tell that the party had already started.

'Whoooie! No kwaito, no party! No girls, no party! No beer, no party!' shouted Themba.

I went inside the house to excuse myself. We had put off leaving for the party until eight o'clock, as Lerato had come up with a brilliant idea. Since food was going to be sold at a buffet at the party, it was better for us to buy it there. There was no need for us to worry about the shops closing down before we bought our spy kos.

As we walked down the street I saw many drunken people of all different ages in a pick-me-up mood. There were cars parked on the pavement all along the street. A couple of drivers had barricaded each end of the street so that it was completely impassable to traffic. The police would have to forget about driving their vans along the street to monitor the jollified crowd.

While some people at one end of the street sat inside their lady-killer sports cars, those who had invested in sound systems were flaunting their large ear-splitting speakers. I am as sure as death that if you had that kind of a sound system in your car most girls wouldn't give a damn about the size of your dick.

Ladies – abantwana, abocherry, abonhwana, abonjunju, abobaby, mantombazane, abosweety, abomysister, abolovey – were prinked in their best tight jeans, hot pants, short dresses and miniskirts, revealing the best that they had.

Drunken guys – amajita, majimbos, amagents, abokawu – were busy harassing the ladies; engaged in endless flirtation in an attempt to procure a victim for a one-night stand.

Everyone was trawling up and down the street searching for the best kwaito music from the parked cars. If Mdu's *Mashamplani* song wasn't humming enough they would go to the other end where B.O.P.'s *Sgiya Ngengoma* was playing. If Thebes's *Sokola Sonke* wasn't to their taste they would quickly turn to another corner where Brenda's *Weekend Special* was pumping.

While eating my spy kos of white bread and fried chips I wondered if the organisers had even bothered to consider their neighbours before planning such a party. I had heard that the party was organised as a six to six celebration. I began to think about the people who would suffer the most in the end, the residents.

Apart from the clatter caused by the gaiety, the residents who lived along that street would be the ones left to clean up the mess while the pig-ignorant organiser would still be sleeping, suffering from babalazi. There was bound to be a carpet of disgusting litter: butts, roaches, used condoms, bottle caps, broken glass, used matchsticks, empty cans, papers and lost keys.

The moans and groans of one-night stands would wake those residents who didn't have a lockable gate. Even those with lockable gates couldn't escape the bottles hurled from drunken partygoers, which might break their windows.

Those who spent their last cents beautifying their gardens might as well resign themselves to finding their gardens stripped of flowers in the morning as the fly-by-night Romeos would have plucked them to charm their willing Juliets.

Dog-lovers were likely to find their animals dead, stabbed with a broken bottle by an angry male party animal who had been trying to invade their yard for kinky sex.

There would be empty bottles and dead bodies in the gardens, blood on the street and rape victims. All this would undoubtedly be followed by endless police interrogations of the innocent homeowners as they tried to locate the wrongdoers.

No one in the township would be surprised by any of this. Those of us who live there know that day in and day out people gad around trying to locate parties. The overwhelming pressure of the environment in which we live makes people pursue their own pleasure at whatever cost. Even if there is no money to spend on a party there are lots of fly-by-night loan sharks called mashonisa. They lend money and hold the borrower's bankcard as a sort of a security. When the borrower gets paid the mashonisa reimburse themselves plus whatever other money is owed to pay off the high interest rate. The bankcard is then returned, irrespective of whether there is any money left on it or not. Sometimes these unregulated and unregistered loan sharks take all of the borrower's salary, no matter how much the borrower owes. It is almost impossible for borrowers to lodge a complaint, and if they go to the mashonisa's business premises the probability is that they will have relocated to an unknown building under a new name.

Most people in the township, from lawyers to spaza shop owners, doctors and street vendors, professionals to laymen, use the mashonisa to overcome their financial problems. Consequently, loan scheme businesses have sprung up all over the township under names such as Affirmative Financers or Freedom Spenders.

It's about time. Listen to Boom Shaka!
Shaka Boom Boom Boom!
Woo! Weee!

The happy crowd sang along to one of the hottest songs by Boom Shaka. I barged into Neo, Theks's brother, who was already drunk. I had a full stomach and was busy on the bottle with my friends. We were standing near the veranda and enjoying the people dancing in the crowd in front of us.

'Hololoo! Are tsamayi rona. Re robala mo! We are not going anywhere. We are sleeping here!' shouted Neo as he joined the dancers.

'Iyo! Yes, yes, yes, baby. Show them, baby! Break that body into pieces! Move that thing. Move it! Wow!' shouted a group of people forming a circle and clapping their hands.

We were all watching Neo who was in the centre of the circle. He was doing an obscene phallocentric dance, wriggling himself like a snake. He grabbed his penis with his right hand at regular intervals to the excitement of the crowd.

An equally drunken girl joined him in that obscene dance, coiling herself tightly around him. She feigned sexual pleasure as Neo repeatedly spanked her almost naked arse with his right hand. There was some whistling from the crowd. Just looking at them my penis hardened as if I was watching pornography with an age restriction of twenty-one. The song ended.

'Some more please! You're great, baby. I just love it,' somebody shouted.

When Mdu's *Tsikitsiki* song started, I was tempted to take the floor. The beer had taken my shyness from me. The dance looked very simple. But as I prepared myself to join the dancing crowd I felt a tap on my shoulders, followed by a kiss on my right cheek. While I was still trying to make sense of that pleasant surprise, some soft arms were flung around me. As she released me, I noticed her beautiful dimples. It was Nkanyezi. Her right hand was holding a bottle of cider. She was wearing a floral miniskirt and a black sleeveless blouse with white stripes that revealed her belly button. She looked wonderful.

'Hi. We meet again,' she said, balancing herself against a pole next to the veranda.

'It's a small world.'

'So. Why are you not dancing?'

'Hmm. I don't have anyone to dance with.'

She smiled broadly.

'Just look at you when you smile. I just love those dimples.'

'Now you are making me shy of myself.'

'Well. It is just that I'm not that easily impressed,' I continued, looking at her. 'But with you babe, there is this spark in me that says that I should honestly tell you how much you are worth. And if I don't I will be gnawed by my guilty conscience.'

Those words left her numb. She didn't know what to say. She took a deep breath. I sipped at my beer. She stared at me for a moment and then gave me a long drunken hug with her head buried in my chest.

All of a sudden Nkanyezi and myself were joined by Themba, who asked where her friend was. At that exact moment Nkanyezi's friend came out of the crowd to join us. She looked exhausted and was soaked with sweat. After greeting me she went and stood with Themba.

'You know I've been thinking about giving you an invitation to my birthday party tomorrow,' said Nkanyezi as she withdrew her warm body from mine.

'Wow! Thanks. You don't know how thrilled I would be to be with a girl like you, especially on such an intimate occasion. But unfortunately I can't come because my ou lady has asked me to accompany her to Pretoria tomorrow,' I lied.

'It's a pity that we only met each other on the eve of my special day. But I hope we'll meet again,' she murmured with concern in her voice.

'Let me give you my contacts before I forget.'

After we had exchanged contact numbers, the two of us chatted about what we were doing in life. I found out that she was a first-year student at Wits Technikon studying electrical engineering. She was not coping well with her studies because she was from a DET school like myself.

She promised to give me a call on Monday and I in turn promised her a belated birthday gift. Although it was hard, I managed to control my penis that night as we held each other tightly. I introduced her to my friends who welcomed her. Then I used the money that I had taken from my aunt to pay the rent at the municipality to buy all of us, including Nkanyezi and her friend, some beers and ciders.

We partied until the wee hours. Around four in the morning we retired, having spent nearly all our money on alcohol, but we were satisfied that we had done our best to celebrate the birth of democracy. The eight of us walked to Dube. We were accompanying the two ladies, Nkanyezi and Tshidi, to their home. We walked in pairs. My left hand was in my pocket, trying to lull my erect penis. That was not its night.

Afterwards we lurched back from Dube, the two of us, Themba and myself, womanless, while Vusi and Dunga continued with their intimate walk. The fun was over.

fifteen

'Dingz, room 229, telephone please!'

A husky muscular voice called my name from the intercom on the second floor of the Y building where I was staying. I was called three times before I answered back.

'Coming.'

'Hurry! The caller is waiting on line three,' commanded the voice.

'OK. I am on my way now.'

I rubbed my eyes, closed my door, and quickly went down to the reception area. There were four telephone lines there. I picked the receiver of line three.

'Heita,' I said, assuming that it was a man who was looking for me.

'Hi, is that Dingz?' a sweet female voice replied from the other end.

'Yeah,' I answered back, curious as to who it could be.

'Hi, you're speaking to Nkanyi.'

'Oh, Nkanyi it's you. It's nice to hear your sweet voice again. Whatsup?'

'I'm OK. What took you so long to answer the phone? You know I nearly ran out of patience. Were you still sleeping?'

I looked at the clock that was mounted on the wall by the vending machine. It was half past nine in the morning. I had missed breakfast. 'Wow, you must be a witch because you're damn right. I was indeed still dreaming.'

'I thought as much.'

'Well, anyway, happy belated birthday to you.'

'Thanks.'

'And how was it? I hope you enjoyed it.'

'Oooh, It was fantastic! I'm sorry for not calling you on Monday to tell you about it.'

'I understand. As long as you had fun it's OK.'

'I hope you still have my birthday present?'

I had forgotten about the promise I had made her. 'Oh yeah. It's waiting for you to collect any time,' I lied.

'What did you get for me?'

'It's a surprise.'

'At least give me a clue.'

'It's something beautiful.'

'That's not a clue.'

'OK then. It weighs five kilos.'

'Well. Never mind. But tell me. Ehh . . .' She paused on the other end of the line. 'Are you in this afternoon; because if you aren't that busy I would like to come pick my gift up around three, on my way home from campus.'

'I can't wait to see you.'

'OK then, I'll call you again when I'm in town. Just wait for my call, will you?'

'I'll look forward to it.'

'OK. Bye for now.'

'Sharp.'

When I returned to my room Dworkin, my roommate, lay on his single bed. I had to break the news to him so that he could give me some privacy when Nkanyi arrived. That was our arrangement when one of us had a female visitor.

Almost every fortnight Dworkin's girlfriend visited him from Vosloorus, his East Rand township home. I often gave them the privacy they needed by going home for the weekend. Sometimes he came back to the Y with ladies I didn't know. Whenever he came with two short loans, as we called them, for a one-night stand, one of them would hook up with me. The four of us would sleep in the same room in what we called a doubleheader. Because of the brotherhood between us it wasn't difficult for me to ask him to come back late from his lectures that afternoon.

'Hey Dwork, remember the new release chick from Soweto that I told you about on Monday?'

'Hmm. Which one?'

'The one that I told you I was with at the street party.'

'Ohoo, I remember now. You mean the one, I told you, that if it were me I would have taken her to bed the very same night!'

'Exactly.'

'What about her?'

'That phone call was from her, my broer, and she is coming over at three this afternoon.'

'Sure? So you want a stadium to play her, izit?'

'You know. That's it, my bra.'

'Don't worry man, I'm actually going to spend some time in the computer lab surfing the Internet this afternoon. I'll come back just before dinner finishes at around eight.'

'That's moja then.'

'But listen, I know women and you must use this chance my bra, otherwise you'll remain friends forever.'

'Sure, pintshi.'

After attending my two lectures I went to the Moosa Supermarket to visit Themba and get some discount goodies for my guest.

Entering my room with my goodies it suddenly came to me that I had forgotten to buy Nkanyi a happy belated birthday card. I was too tired to go to the shops again, and besides, the sun was hot up there. I decided to improvise.

I knew that Dworkin was also known as Sakhi back home, and he had a collection of old birthday cards from his many girlfriends. I began to ransack his bookshelves searching for a birthday card that still looked new. Although most of them were already dog-eared, I was lucky to find one with the following inscription in capital letters.

DEAREST SAKHI

I THINK IT'S BEST TO LET YOU KNOW THAT SOMEONE LOVES
AND CARES ABOUT YOU . . . AND THAT SOMEONE IS ME.

HAPPY BIRTHDAY.
WITH ALL MY LOVE

DINEO

The card was perfect. But I still had to add a few words to make
it more appealing to my guest. Carefully, I blotted out the name
Sakhi with Tipp-Ex and wrote *Nkanyi* instead. Where it read
Dineo, I carefully Tipp-Exed over the vowels *e* and *o* and wrote *gz*,
so that the name read as *Dingz*. I also added something of my
own:

PS. I'M SORRY FOR NOT BEING THERE TO
CELEBRATE THIS IMPORTANT EVENT WITH
THE MOST BEAUTIFUL GIRL I HAVE SEEN.

After I had completed my dishonest act, I slipped the card inside
an envelope, lay down on my bed and switched on my radio to kill
time while I waited for her call.

At about half past two I started to become impatient. I got up
from my bed and sprayed some air-freshener around the room. I
then loaded the only two chairs available in the room with papers and books. Dworkin had given me that tip. He had said that
she must not have any other choice upon her arrival but to sit on
my bed. On my small table I put my old tape recorder that I had
borrowed from home. I selected some music that I thought Nkanyi would love to listen to and put the cassettes next to the tape
recorder.

I sat down on my bed again and began to search through the
many almost-identical radio stations for a pleasing melody. After

I had succeeded in my search, I started to read through a recent issue of the *Drum* magazine. But my mind was not capable of concentrating on the magazine. I looked at my wristwatch. I wished she would call immediately.

At about twenty past three Nkanyi called for me from our reception area. Nervously, I walked down to the reception. She was sitting on the sofa wading through an old issue of *You* magazine. She was wearing a floral print dress, a thin gold necklace and bracelet as well as large circular gold earrings.

'Hi sweetie,' I said.

'Hi,' she replied shyly.

We hugged; I held her warm body and felt her soft lips as she kissed me hello. Her hand clasped mine for a brief moment and my body temperature rose quickly. I felt like my whole body was already inside her.

I had to whisk her out of the reception area before the caretaker saw me. No female visitor was ever allowed beyond the reception area. That was our number-one rule and it was non-negotiable.

As soon as I opened the door to the stairs the caretaker called my name. I knew that I was in hot water for trying to bend the rules. Before going to the caretaker, I asked Nkanyi to wait for me by the door.

'What do you think you are doing?' he asked out of Nkanyi's earshot.

'Please, my bra,' I said shyly.

'You know you can't take a lady to your room.'

'But she is my sister, man.'

'You can't fool me. I saw the way you hugged.'

'Were you spying on us?'

'Those are the rules.'

'Rules are merely guidelines about behaviour, man. They are not meant to be applied rigidly against your black brother,' I replied playfully.

'But you know I'm on duty and if I let you go with her I'll lose my job.'

'I promise it will be a quick thing; she won't stay for long, man.'

The caretaker slowly shook his head.

'You're trouble, you know that?'

'You know,' I said, shrugging my shoulders.

'This would be at your own risk. You never saw me and never talked to me.'

'My lips are sealed.' I drew my fingers across my mouth.

'Be careful. The Priest is very concerned about us relaxing the rules.'

'I will, man,' I said as I grabbed Nkanyi by the hand and scuttled towards my room.

Once inside my room, we both sat on my single bed and looked at her birthday pictures.

'Can I offer you something to drink?' I asked.

'That would be super. I really feel hot.'

'How hot?' I asked suggestively.

'Very.'

'Will red grape juice be OK for you?' I asked as I opened the small residence refrigerator.

'Oh boy, that's my favourite.'

'Izit?'

I took two tall glasses out of my cupboard and poured juice into them both. I handed one full glass to her. I then took a dinner plate that I had stolen from the dining hall the other day and emptied a packet of snacks onto it. I snuggled down beside her on my bed and watched her as she threw a snack into her mouth, then crunched it slowly between her milk-white teeth. Although there was no direct eye contact between us, she could see out of the corner of her right eye that I was watching her as she dug into the snacks. She pretended to be concentrating on the *Drum* magazine. I looked at her sharp breasts underneath her floral dress. I started seething inwardly; I didn't have courage to continue from where I had left off the other night.

Out of the blue she started smiling; her long forefinger on her right hand was tracing a sentence in the magazine. Nosily, I peered across at the magazine to share the joke. She was reading the horoscopes; her finger hovered over Taurus. It read:

> **Taurus:** *April 21 – May 21* – Make yourself irresistible by being amorous. This could be a spellbinding session of romance if you grasp your chance to impress your true love, or attract someone very special.

Nkanyi looked at me and smiled broadly.

'What's your star sign?' she asked with great curiosity.

I wasn't a great fan of horoscopes. I could never recognise anything that resembled my life in what they told me. Besides, the other day when I had told Theks that I was a Gemini she had told me a lot of nonsense about that star sign. She had sworn that she would never go out with a Gemini because we were an unpredictable bunch of people. She said they have two selves and that was why I was a moody person. According to Theks, Geminis are not easy to live with because one day we are caring and nice and the next day we are very bad.

'Do you believe in horoscopes?' I asked while quickly scanning what was written about Gemini in the magazine.

'I think they are about eighty percent right in most cases.'

'Is that so?'

'Yeah, I think so,' she said doubtfully.

I finished reading about my star sign. I was pleased with what I had read; there was no reason for me to lie at all.

'Actually I am a Gemini.'

'Let's see then.' She began to read my horoscope out loud.

> **Gemini:** *May 21 – June 22* – Love has a very nice vibration to it now. Make a special effort to be more loving and plan

ahead if your relationship is to be strong.

'Wow, that sounds very real,' I said helping myself to some snacks.

'I didn't think you'd believe in horoscopes.'

'That part I do believe in.'

'What part?'

'The part about love and vibration,' I said, 'especially when sitting with a gorgeous lady like yourself with a beautiful smile.' I accidentally touched her right thigh with my left leg.

She smiled broadly and exposed her dimples. She saw that I was watching her and covered her dimples with her hands, but continued smiling.

'You always have something nice to say to me, don't you?'

'Now I know what made me sleep badly the other night when we parted,' I whispered to her.

'What?'

'It's because I was afraid of asking you if I could touch those dimples.' I raised my hand to touch her smooth cheek.

She didn't speak or try to prevent me from touching her. Her immobility challenged me to be more romantic. I thought that I had finally found the courage that I needed. I maintained eye contact as I slowly drew my face towards hers. The need of her was running through my body. Our lips steadily met half-way. We tentatively kissed. Her lips tasted like fresh grapes. I reached for her breast. She lifted my T-shirt and stroked my back with a long caress. I lifted her dress took it off over her head. Within a minute my T-shirt was off as well.

After that everything was spontaneous. Our wet tongues snaked together. My jeans were on the floor. I had already taken leave of my senses and forgotten that there was a thing called a condom as I reached for the heaven that lay between her legs. Breast to breast and pelvis to pelvis we both gasped with pleasure. I found her clitoral peak. I heard her gasping. She pressed me harder on her as we finally reached the earthly paradise of sexual climax. I couldn't stop at that moment, not even if there had been an intruder in my room with an axe ready to chop me into mincemeat. I would rather have died on top of her.

I felt my penis waning and withdrew. I watched her stash away her voluptuous body inside her dress. As soon as she had finished, she opened the refrigerator and took out the grape juice. I was only half dressed, and as I bent over to carefully remove my jeans that had somehow managed to get stuck underneath my bed, I saw an open box of free condoms that I had collected from the campus clinic the previous month. That sight of condoms brought me back to my senses again. Quietly, I started blaming myself for putting myself under unnecessary stress. All I could hear were the echoes of my own mind, where one prominent scary voice that I wished to suppress was saying to me:

TOO LATE. YOU HAVE ALREADY SUCCUMBED TO THE WORLD, THE FLESH AND THE DEVIL.

I silently put on my jeans and flopped down on my bed beside her. I swallowed the juice that she had just poured into my glass. I held her hand and gave her a kiss directly on her dimples. I gave her another quick kiss on the back of her right hand.

'By the way, where is my birthday gift?' she asked.

I had forgotten about the gift.

'I already gave it to you,' I answered without thinking.

'No you didn't.'

'Yes I did,' I insisted playfully.

'Maybe you are suffering from forgetfulness.'

'Nope.'

'When did you give me your gift then?'

'When we had a great time and you were screaming with pleasure.'

'Was that your gift?'

'Oh yeah. Remember you never asked me what sort of a gift I had for you.'

'Whatever,' she said, chuckling.

There was a moment of silence between us. I caressed her right thigh. She lifted my T-shirt to caress my back.

'Stop it,' she said spanking my arse to prevent me from going any further.

'Just once more.'

'No. I have to go,' she said, raising herself from the bed.

She looked at the time on her gold wristwatch. It was twenty minutes past five in the afternoon. 'Jeez. My train is at twenty to. Can you take me to Park Station?'

I stood up and opened my drawer to get her birthday card. She read it and gave me a long tight hug, followed by a quick kiss on my cheek.

'I love the words, Dingz. Do you really mean them?' she asked with her hands around my neck.

'Oh yes, sweetheart. They come from deep down in this big heart of mine,' I answered, thumping my chest with my right hand.

'I love you too, Dingz.'

She released her warm body from mine and slipped the card between the books in her schoolbag. I opened the door and we walked to Park Station together.

It was the beginning. She was officially mine.

sixteen

'O-one. T-two. Th-three. Down-dow-wn go! Dow-wn dow-wn go! Down do-wn go! Down-down do-wnn gooo! Hoo-rah!'

We were in the Dropout bar on Jorissen Street in Braamfontein. A multiracial group of drunken students were shouting and clapping their hands, encouraging a black girl who was wearing a lilac sweater to drink a large jug full of Castle Draught without taking a break. A white girl was holding down her left hand.

The five of us – Themba, Dworkin, Babes, Theks and myself – were sitting in our usual spot on the two long green leather-clad benches. Dwork, Babes and myself were facing the pool tables and the table soccer opposite the toilet. The rest of my drinking crew were facing the large television screen behind us. Between us was a table covered in beer bottles.

The group we were watching consisted of about eight people: two black guys, one black girl who was busy drinking, three white girls, one Indian guy and one white guy. The Indian guy was slapping his hand on the table as the rest of that group counted from one to ten. It was as if he was the referee in a wrestling match.

The Dropout bar exploded with the sound of applause as the girl finished the whole jug of Castle Draught. The bar owner flashed his deceitful smile as the girl coughed three times with her fist against her mouth to clear her throat, then raised both of her clenched fists and thumped them down three times on the table.

'Yes! Yes! Yes! Hhu! Whoeieeei,' she shouted, looking around as if to see whether her achievement was being fully appreciated by the other heavy drinkers.

'Iiiiyo! The world is a stage, and everyone is an actor, my friend,' said Themba when I looked surprised at the girl's performance.

'Com' on!' shouted the bar owner, starting to clap his hands. 'Let's give her another big round of applause.'

Writhing in delight, the girl struggled to stand up and take a bow.

'Welcome to S.A.D.U. – our very own and newly formed South African Drinkers Union,' cried Themba.

'People, isn't she wonderful?' said her phuza-faced Indian friend.

'Yeah! Yeah! Yeah! I love you. You're the best baby. I'm taking you home tonight,' someone shouted.

Suddenly the music from the jukebox was switched off and the bald-headed white bar owner rang the bell for silence. He clambered up onto the counter.

'I thank you all for supporting Dropout this evening. But a special thanks to Ntombi here,' he said. 'She has kept us entertained with her brilliant performance. She has shown us how to enjoy life to the full.'

Another round of applause followed. 'Today is also a special day because it's her birthday; let's all sing for her.'

'Happy birthday to you. Happy birthday to you. Happy birthday dear Ntombi. Happy birthday to you.' Our voices echoed around the bar.

'Hip hip,' shouted the Indian guy.

'Hoorah!' the crowd responded.

The bar owner rang his bell again and silence followed. 'Dropout would like to award Ntombi with an honorary degree for putting on a brilliant performance,' he said, signalling the bartender to fill another jug of Castle Draught.

'We are happy to announce that Ntombi is now officially a BA. For those who don't know a BA stands for Bachelor of Alcohol here at the Dropout and each day for a week Ntombi will be given a jug of Castle Draught. So far only Mr Naidoo here has our highest honorary degree, the LLB.' The owner pointed at the Indian guy who had acted as the referee earlier on. 'An LLB here at the Dropout stands for Bachelor of Liquors and means that he doesn't have to pay the cover charge for coming in here or the ten rand deposit to use the white ball for the pool table. I hope you enjoy the rest of the night and thank you.'

The bar owner climbed down from the counter and smiled at Ntombi. She smiled back broadly at him and whispered a heartfelt 'thank you' under her breath.

On the wall above the bar owner's shining shaven head was a big poster with a man holding a glass of beer:

NEVER TRUST A MAN WHO DOES NOT DRINK

The inscription at the bottom read:

ONE MAN ONE TOT

One black guy from Ntombi's table stood up and walked to the jukebox. He put some coins in the slot and Brenda's old jam started to hum: 'Hello weekend. Weekend special'.

'Can anyone here tell me how the president of the S.A.D.U. lost the election during the festive season? I'll buy you a case of beer right now if you can tell me,' said Themba, as if such an organisation really existed.

'Nobody knows. Tell us,' said Babes enthusiastically, not wasting any time.

'All right then, you all lose. Let me tell you. You know S.A.D.U. elections are held annually in a bar like this one. So, last season the elections were held in a bar near to my home. Five contestants were lined up; they were all heavy drinkers with phuza faces like that guy over there.' He paused and pointed at the Indian guy with his finger. 'The bar owner introduced the candidates to the crowd before the elections took place. He then lined up fifteen glasses on the table, each one filled with a different brand of alcohol. The candidates were then blindfolded and each one of them had to take a sip from each glass and identify the alcohol by its

116

taste. Whoever got the highest score would be made president of the union.' He paused and took a sip from his glass.

'So what if they all identified all fifteen of those glasses?' asked Dworkin, struggling to control his laughter.

'Wait! That's the interesting part I'm coming to,' ordered Themba, raising his hand.

Silence fell around our table and Themba continued. 'It started with Gusheshe, the current president with a real phuza face from Zola section. He took the first glass and sipped it.' Themba acted the sipping of a glass. 'He curled his lips pompously, clicked his tongue and shouted, "Castle; brewed in 1895 to give you the greatest taste, contains 5% alcohol!" The crowd roared with applause. He then lifted the second glass and shouted, "Hansa Pilsner; to our soil all the way from Czechoslovakia, contains 4.5% alcohol". After the third glass he shouted, "Black Label, America's lusty beer, 5.5% alcohol". Fourth was a rosé wine and he was even confident enough to say semi-sweet. After the fifth glass he shouted, "Ahhhh! Umqombothi; our very own South African pride from amabela".'

Babes' tomboyish face was beaming with suppressed laughter. Her thick black lips were trembling uncontrollably. She stretched her thin neck forward. I could see two bulging veins in it. 'So . . .' she began, trying to control her laughter, 'this guy wasn't the president of S.A.D.U. for nothing. He knew his stuff,' she managed to say as she dabbed the corners of her eyes with her stumpy long-nailed fingers.

'Yeah. As I said he was a well-known drinker in the township and a history teacher in one of the high schools in Soweto.'

'Iyooo! A teacher?' asked Theks, disappointedly.

'Yes, a history teacher,' confirmed Themba.

'And what happened next?' I asked.

'So after fifteen glasses the result was a draw. Ten more glasses were added. But in the last glass there was only water; just pure water from the tap. So the president sipped the first nine glasses and identified them all. But after sipping the tenth one he paused and scratched his head. Remember that the rule was that they were blindfold, so they couldn't see the colour of the alcohol inside each glass. After straining to recollect anything from his alcohol-addled memory about the brand in the tenth and final glass, in the very last round of that decisive election he finally said, "This is a new brand of alcohol I've never tasted before in my life".'

We all laughed as hard as we could.

When the laughter had subsided Dworkin asked, 'So that's how the stupid president lost the elections?'

'As simple as that, my friend. Now the president is Thibos, the guy from Cancer, and he's got a real phuza face,' replied Themba.

The bartender came over to our table and collected some empty bottles. We ordered another four beers. As the bartender picked up the last empty bottle, Dworkin's eyes landed on two gorgeous coloured girls who were busy playing pool. His eyes followed the one who was wearing a revealing orange miniskirt. The girl walked around the pool table to make some calculation on the angle. As she bent over to make the shot, Dworkin whistled under his breath.

'Hhuu! Whoieeie! All things bright and beautiful, madoda,' he said, nudging me for attention.

'I guess you're already hard, Dwork?' said Babes, smiling at Dwork. 'How long have you been staring at her?'

'Ooooh! Me? Ha, ha,' laughed Dworkin mockingly. 'That's nothing. I've dated beautiful women. Real women, not ones you find in a bar like this,' he said boastfully, still staring at the two girls. 'These ones have already expired. I'm talking about Miss Soweto, Miss Pretoria and Miss North West.'

'Whaaa! And where are they now?' asked Theks contemptuously.

'Ag!' he exclaimed curtly. 'I've jilted them all.'

'Not that they've jilted you?' snapped Theks.

'I'm imagining a chicken-hearted fool like you dating a Miss

Soweto and I think in your dreams?' added Babes with indignation in her voice.

'Let me leave you retards alone,' said Dworkin. He turned away from Babes and Theks and began to whisper to me. 'You see Dingz? That's what we call a gorgeous woman, not these two depressingly ugly girls we are drinking with.' Theks shot a curious look at us as we talked.

'Are you sure he is not masturbating under the table?' she asked me.

'Don't worry! As soon as there's a funny smell I'll let you know that side,' I replied.

'Oh boy! I'm thinking of going over there now to try my luck,' said Dworkin, chewing on his matchstick.

'I would give it a try right now if I were you. She's kick-ass, man,' Themba encouraged him.

'Ho! Guys, you must be careful nowadays,' warned Babes.

'Why should we?'

'Because AIDS kills, my boy,' answered Babes.

'Nonsense,' said Themba. 'Don't you know that circumcised straight men never catch the gay plague?' He looked down and poured another glass of beer for himself. 'Only the kwenkwes do,' he concluded jokingly.

As Themba put down the beer I picked it up to refill my glass as well. But to my surprise it was already empty. I opened another one with my teeth.

'Aaagg suka wena! You don't even know what a circumcision school looks like,' snapped Dworkin.

'Eintlik, yes I do,' insisted Themba. 'They amputate your foreskin there,' he said making a gesture with both his forefingers.

'Voetsek! Liar. There is no such school in Soweto or any other township!'

'What do you mean there are no circumcision schools in the townships?' asked Themba. 'What about the Langa circumcision school, out along the N2, near the airport in Cape Town? Didn't

119

you watch the TV news about a week ago when seven of the boys were taken to hospital because they fell ill? Or is Langa not a township anymore?' he asked, flinging his arms wide and thrusting his head forward with his eyes wide open.

'Imagine, Langa suburb,' teased Babes. 'Truly speaking, arsehole, the two words just don't go together.'

Raising both his hands to acknowledge Themba's point, Dworkin replied. 'OK. OK. OK. All right then. I agree you can find a circumcision school in the townships. But that doesn't mean we should talk about our ancient and noble tradition like . . .' He paused to receive the cigarette that I had been smoking and had passed to him. He puffed at it, swallowed the smoke and prepared to continue. 'Because I think . . .'

'Whatever,' interrupted Theks, not giving Dworkin a chance to finish. 'That old-fashioned tradition of yours is still creeping in the heart of darkness and should be brought to the light of modernity.' She paused. 'It's doing more harm than good in the community nowadays.'

'What do you mean it causes harm to the community?' I said.

Theks shook her head slowly. 'Look! I mean nowadays there is the question of HIV and AIDS. Just imagine the illiterate traditional doctors, who use one unsterilised razor blade to amputate the foreskins of hundreds of people.' She contorted her face as if she had just swallowed something bitter.

'Yerrrrr! Who told you that nonsense? For your information the circumcision school doctors use a different razor for each person; the family of the initiate has to supply their own blade. Do you think that our traditional rites of passage should be forsaken in favour of those of the whites? Do you favour waiting until you turn twenty-one to celebrate your passage into adulthood with that stupid key?' snapped Dworkin, stubbing out the butt of his cigarette.

'I think that's better than the amputation of your foreskin, don't you, Theks,' replied Themba, glancing at Theks.

'Chill, guys.' I interrupted before Theks could defend herself. 'What the bush schools need to improve on is their medical training. The traditional doctors need to be armed with knowledge about the spread of the HIV virus.'

A moment of silence followed. Themba stared at nothingness on the ceiling.

'Do you also believe in that AIDS shit?' asked Dworkin, looking at me disappointedly. He was playing with the matchstick in his mouth. 'Do you even know what AIDS stands for?'

'Yessus! What a stupid question! Of course, we all do, man. Who doesn't?' replied Themba, rubbing his temple. 'Ag man, I mean everybody knows that it stands for Acquired Immune Deficiency Syndrome.'

'Wrong answer. Anyone else?' said Dworkin, as if he was our primary school teacher.

There was grumbling around the table as we protested. Babes lit up another cigarette to help her mull over Dworkin's question. Themba and myself took sips from our respective glasses.

'So, no one knows?' asked Dworkin, shaking his dreadlocks. 'Well, boys and girls,' he began with a mock smile. 'For your information, the acronym AIDS stands for "American Invention for Discouraging Sex", or in a more scholarly form "Academic Imaginary Death Sentence".' He paused for a second and looked around the table. 'It was fabricated to marginalize the illiterate and the poor.' After taking another sip from his glass he continued his lecture. 'The rich and the arrogant are conniving with the academics against the poor and the ignorant so that they will be the only ones able to enjoy the worldly paradise of sex.' He rubbed his thumb between the forefinger and the middle finger of the same hand. 'And they do that by scaring us away from that activity through this AIDS shit.'

We all laughed loudly. We knew that everything Dworkin said had to be taken with a pinch of salt. He was a well-known fabricator of weird stories and he also enjoyed arguing just for the sake of it.

When I lifted the quart to pour a beer, I found that it was already finished. The bartender was taking his time coming over to our table to collect the empty bottles and give us another round. Ma Willies' *Into Enjani Leyo*, which was pumping on the jukebox, made any attempt to call for service pointless. Since it was my round, I felt that I should not keep my friends scratching their throats for long. I stood up and went to the bar.

About eight or nine people stood at the counter, waiting for their turn to buy drinks from the two bartenders, as well as one of the gorgeous coloured chicks that Dworkin had taken a fancy to earlier on.

Ntombi, the girl who had graduated into the world of drinkers earlier that evening, was sleeping with her mouth wide open at the table next to Mr Naidoo. The rest of the people at the table were drunkenly singing along with Ma Willies.

I stood next to the coloured girl by the counter waiting to be served. I glanced at her, then peered back at our table to see if Dworkin was watching me. Our eyes locked. Cautiously I took my left hand from the counter and pretended to spank her butt. She soon noticed that I was smiling, so I pretended to be amused by the notices that were written in black ink just above the spirits behind the bar.

**TO BE CONSIDERED FOR CREDIT,
YOU MUST BE 96 YEARS OF AGE OR OLDER,
WITH A COMPLETE DENTAL FORMULA
AND MUST BE ACCOMPANIED BY
BOTH PARENTS, ALL CARRYING YOUR ID'S.**

And:

**BANKS DON'T GIVE BEER CREDIT SO DON'T
EVEN BOTHER TO ASK FOR IT IN THIS BAR.**

Those notices were familiar to me; I always saw them each time I visited the bar. The girl looked at me and smiled.

'I always read that notice every time I come here, I think it's nice.'

'I think so too,' I agreed.

With a smile pasted on her lips the girl pointed at another notice next to the wineglasses. 'But look at the one up there man, I think it's the most amusing,' she said.

Pretending that I hadn't seen the notice before, I read it out loud.

PLEASE HELP SAVE WATER BY DRINKING BEER

I feigned amusement, but by then it was the girl's turn to be served. I looked back at our table and realised that Dworkin had been watching us all along. Jealously he flung both his hands out with his mouth half-open, as if accusing me of chatting up his chick. I pretended to be moving my hand across the girl's behind as she reached across the bar to take her order.

After placing my order I staggered back to our table with six more quarts of Castle Lager. My crew was still arguing about AIDS.

'Ek sê, Dwork, but even if it stands for that, it still kills,' growled Themba. Babes and Theks shrugged their approval to back him up.

'Oh wé! You are misinformed, my friends,' said Dwork. 'It is not that AIDS is incurable, but that the Americans are making money out of this disease by making you believe that it is.'

'Tell them, brother,' I shouted to encourage him.

'OK then. Don't just make claims without backing them up. Tell us how they do that,' demanded Babes, picking up her beer.

'OK then, chill, sister!' said Dworkin. 'And let me break down this mystery and shed the light in your small, dark, alcohol-addled brain forever and ever. The Americans are making it difficult for poor South Africans to procure the drugs they need by making them expensive. In fact, your right to life is being tampered with here. And the reason they are doing this, if you want to know, is nothing more than economic fundamentalism. I wonder if you understand that. Of course if you're an AIDS sufferer and want to live longer you will have to buy those expensive medicines.'

'Ohoo!' said Babes half-heartedly, curling her lip. 'Now you are being a mythomaniac again.'

'You mean you don't know that if you rely on those cheap fong-kong condoms they burst in the middle of an orgasm?' asked Dworkin. 'Well, I don't blame you, I know you're starving yourself these days. You're such a stingy arsehole when it comes to spreading your ugly legs apart for us to dance between,' he said, hunching forward with his elbows on the table. 'Let me tell you something you don't know.' He looked Babes deep in the eye and his voice became almost a whisper. 'Only the bourgeois can afford the Lovers Plus condoms, my dear. And where does that leave us? In other words, the academics and bourgeois are telling us that if you're rich, go to the nearest whorehouse and fuck any prostitute in the world and you will still live longer. But if you're poor you are at great risk of contracting their disease because you are bound to use the cheap fong-kong condoms supplied through the beneficence of the rich bureaucrats.'

'So, in other words, are you saying that sex has become the social activity of the rich while AIDS is a discriminatory disease of the poor?' asked Themba.

'You're very right my friend. Absolutely yes.'

Dworkin paused and ruffled his dreadlocked hair. He adjusted the matchstick he was still busy chewing. 'And that's why when America sneezes the rest of the world experiences an economic slump, but when the White House bonks Africa catches an STD.'

We all laughed loudly. I extended my hand to Dworkin and shouted. 'Give me five, boy!'

'But guys, I read something in the paper suggesting that you

South African black males have exhausted all the possible help the world can come up with,' began Babes.

'What do you mean?' enquired Themba.

'Well. I think you all know that our government imports its condoms from China.' We all nodded. 'Currently we are importing condoms which are about this big,' she said smiling as she stretched apart her thumb and forefinger. 'Although those condoms are much bigger than the sizes exported to the rest of the world, it was reported that our government have asked the Chinese manufacturers to make even bigger ones because African dicks are much bigger than the rest of the world.' Babes' lips parted for a smile and I could see the small gap between her front teeth.

'So what's your point?' asked Themba impatiently.

'Hello! I mean, can't you see the logic here?' she asked, trying to hide the smile on her face. 'Even if you were supplied with expensive condoms, your dicks are so big that they would break them.'

'Anyway what do you expect from China. Those guys only sell fong-kongs,' concluded Themba.

'Let's not concern ourselves with this AIDS shit,' said Dworkin casually. 'We're all going to die at the end of the day, whether we're HIV or not.'

'Ek sê, my bra. Please leave me your PC in your will, man,' I said to Dworkin.

'Who said I wanna die? Or do you wanna kill me?' said Dworkin, suddenly looking scared.

'Have you seen how full Avalon cemetery is nowadays?' asked Themba. 'Very soon we'll be burying our dead in our own backyards like they used to do long ago.'

'Or cremate people like they are proposing in Kwazulu,' added Theks.

'Which reminds me, Dwork, that if you were from my Shangaan culture, and died without having been married, we would

125

shove a maize cob in your stinking arse and bury you during the week to show that you were worthless,' I said contemptuously.

'Mind your language!' warned Dworkin, while the rest laughed.

'Sis! Fuck your culture,' swore Babes, wrinkling her nose.

'But does that still apply?' asked Dworkin, pretending not to have taken offence at what I had said.

'No. Your modernity has destroyed that practice.'

Themba shouted another round as soon as the bartender came to collect some empty bottles from our table. 'Give us six more,' he said, handing a fifty rand banknote to the bartender.

'I can see you're determined to hit the bottle tonight,' said Babes.

'Don't forget you're working this morning,' warned Theks.

I looked at my wristwatch and it was already ten minutes past one. 'Do you guys know where AIDS started and how?' asked Themba after sipping his beer.

'I read it started somewhere in Central Africa in the late 1960s, if I'm not mistaken. Somewhere in the Congo,' answered Babes.

'No. Why do you have to travel that far? The disease started in Soweto in the early 1980s,' said Themba.

'So-we-to?' we all said simultaneously.

'Yes, Soweto as in Soweto.'

'What is the basis of your lie?' questioned Dworkin.

'Listen! This is not a joke and I'm sure Dingz knows the story as well,' began Themba. 'In the early 1980s there was a succubus called Vera the Ghost.' He looked at me and I nodded, although I didn't have a clue what he was talking about. 'She was a man-eater. She was capable of creating the illusion that guys were sleeping with a really beautiful woman, in a queen-sized bed, in a five-star hotel. The next day the men would wake to find themselves naked and covered with ash on top of a grave in Avalon cemetery.'

'Ha! That's another urban legend,' Dworkin laughed.

'It's the truth, man!' insisted Themba. 'Guys in the township opted to abstain from sex because of the fear of Vera the Ghost. You see, she would walk the streets of Soweto looking for hunks with muscles and six-packs. In the . . .'

'I guess you must have survived because you didn't fit the criteria,' Theks interrupted, using her hand to show Themba's round beer belly.

Laughter followed.

'At least my face is still youthful and not expired like yours because of beer and sexual starvation,' retaliated Themba.

More laughter. 'As I was saying, people, before I was interrupted, Vera was the kind of woman you couldn't pass on the street without looking. Once she chose a guy, everybody at the party would envy the lucky hunk. But after the party, boom, the hunk would be lured to her grave at Avalon cemetery,' concluded Themba.

'Oh weee! Where do you get this crap from?' asked Babes.

'She is the one who started infecting people with AIDS because she was so mad at Sowetans after she was raped on the street one night.'

'Ohooo! So it was revenge?' asked Dworkin.

We waited with our mouths agape for Themba, who was busy taking a drink, to finish his story. Our eyes followed his hand. He didn't look at us, but carefully wiped his mouth and smiled at his ability to keep us in suspense.

'One day she was walking the street somewhere in Cancer on her lookout for a hunk to appease her insatiable sexual appetite. About five guys lured her away from the party. She didn't offer any resistance when they dragged her into the reeds by a stream and gang-raped her. When they were finished with her they wanted to run away so that she didn't have a chance of recognising them. But before they could leave she stood up, dusted herself off slowly and whispered, "Thank you for the wonderful night". After kissing each one of them she disappeared. The poor guys were so happy and surprised it didn't even click that she wasn't a human being but a succubus. The following day they were all taken ill with a deadly syphilis that developed into HIV. So that's how it happened. HIV-AIDS from the succubus called Vera the Ghost.'

We were silent for a little while. Chicco's old jam, *We Miss You Manellow* was playing on the jukebox.

'Do you still want her?' Babes asked Dworkin, referring to the coloured girl he had the hots for.

'Iiiiiyo! Do you think she is a succubus?' I asked.

'Ooh!' Theks shrugged her shoulders. 'You won't know until you try it.'

'Theks is just jealous; go for it, Dwork,' Themba encouraged him.

'Do it yourself,' replied Dworkin.

Theks's eyes were suddenly fixed on the main door; we could tell that someone had just entered the bar. Silence followed. I knew that we had found something to divert us from the AIDS topic.

'Whutsup now, guys?' asked Dworkin nosily.

'It's those two Kiwi-black Shangaans,' whispered Theks under her breath.

'They are not even black, they're navy blue,' corrected Themba.

'Black is beautiful, don't you know that by now,' interrupted Babes.

'Ha!' Theks exclaimed mockingly. 'There is nothing beautiful about that black.'

Dworkin, Themba and myself turned to look behind us before we missed the action, but all I could see was Tawanda our Zimbabwean classmate approaching. With him was his Ethiopian friend, Mohammed. I didn't know Mohammed that well, although I had met him several times before, but Tawanda was my friend and I knew that he was Shona. We had nicknamed him T-Man. If he were indeed a Shangaan I would've been able to communicate with him, as I sucked that language from my mother's breasts. We had been speaking English all night, as we were a little United Nations, and it would have been a pleasant opportunity for me to speak to him in Shangaan. While Tawanda and Mohammed were still busy exchanging greetings with two guys sitting on the stools by the bar, I turned to Theks.

'Just for the record, let me break the xenophobic darkness in your damaged brains, my sister. T-Man is Shona and not Shangaan.'

'Ha! What's the difference?' snapped Theks. 'They all eat mopane worms and locusts and he is black like Kiwi polish. Besides, they all jabber in the same dialect.'

'Does the word Shangaan nowadays mean every person who has a dark complexion and speaks a language that is foreign to your stupid ears? For your information, the Shangaan language is one of the eleven official languages in South Africa, it is also an official language in Mozambique, and although there are some Shangaan people in Zimbabwe, T-Man is definitely not one of them,' I said, and excused myself to wobble to the ladies to take a pee.

When I came back from the toilet Mohammed and T-Man were already seated at our table, and the bartender had arranged two more glasses for them. Mohammed's glass was filled with some Coca-Cola and ice cubes.

'Oh T-Man, my bra, howzit?' I greeted Tawanda.

'Sharp, my bra.'

'Hey! Don't shake his hand, he's just come from the ladies,' warned Babes playfully.

'For Christ sake. I didn't use my hand to wipe my arse like you do.'

'But did you wash your hands?' snapped Theks.

'And also dried them, asshole.'

'Oh weee!' said Babes sarcastically.

I turned to greet Mohammed.

'Salaam alaikum.'

'Wa-alaikum salaam,' he answered smiling.

The others all laughed, but I ignored them and sat between Mohammed and T-Man.

'Man. I didn't know you were Shona,' said Theks, looking at T-man.

'What did you think I was?' asked T-Man in his strong Zimbabwean accent.

The bartender came to collect the six empty bottles from our table. Before Theks could answer, T-Man gave the bartender a fifty rand note. 'Bring us five more of those please.'

'Coming just now,' replied the bartender as he scurried away with the empty bottles.

'I thought you were a Nigerian or something.'

'And why would you think that?'

'Oh! Just a guess, that's all.'

'Anyway. Dingz and Dwork know me very well.'

'You have two ethnic groups there, Shona and Ndebele, isn't it?' interrupted Babes, sipping her beer.

'Not really, there are a lot of ethnic groups, just like here in South Africa. There are the Lozis from Zambia, Kalangas, Shangaans, Afrikaners, English and Chewas. It's just that Shona and Ndebele are the official languages.'

Eight more beer bottles arrived. I opened two of them by using another bottle. Every body except Mohammed and Theks poured beer into their glasses. Theks was already yawning. Themba slumbered in his seat at regular intervals.

'Guys, I think I can call it a day. I'm really drunk and I can't risk any more after this glass,' protested Babes, yawning.

'Aaaaaaaaaaa!' yawned Themba. 'That makes the two of us.'

I was drunk as well. The multiracial tribe that had been singing at the table beside us had long gone. It was now about quarter to three in the morning.

'What's your fucken time?' asked Babes, swaying unsteadily from side to side.

130

'Already fourteen minutes to fuck you!' replied Dworkin.

'Iiiiiiyo! In your dreams. I may be drunk, but I'm not drunk enough to share a bed with you.'

'I'm serious.'

'You wish. Over my dead body.'

'Are you sure?'

'Whatever. Guys I think there is always a next time,' said Babes as she raised herself from the chair and gulped the last of her beer. She shook Themba who was already snoring noisily. 'Wake up you amateur, before you have your wet dream here.'

'Guys, we'll see you, enjoy the rest of the morning' I said to Mohammed, Dwork and T-Man, who were still busy drinking. The rest of us lurched towards the door.

'Cheers, guys,' they replied simultaneously. 'Rest in peace all of you arseholes,' added Dworkin.

'Fuck you too,' said Themba.

seventeen

On Saturday morning I was woken up by the intercom again. I was not expecting any visitors and I was suffering from a serious hangover from the previous night's drinking spree. I rubbed my eyes to remove some sleep. *It can't be Nkanyi*; the caller had used my full name: Dingamanzi. That was unusual.

So who was it? I knew that it was not one of my friends or family members. I looked at the alarm clock on my desk. It was half past eleven; I had already missed breakfast. I dressed quickly and walked down to the reception area, not bothering to brush my teeth.

In reception, one of the caretakers on duty referred me to the Priest's office. Apparently he was the person who wanted to have a word with me. The last time I was in the Priest's office was during our so-called hunger strike; I had been given a suspension for inciting the other residents. I was told that I shouldn't be found guilty of any other offence for at least three months, otherwise my place at the Y would be in jeopardy. Those three months had not elapsed yet, but that particular morning I convinced myself that surely I had done nothing wrong. There was no reason to panic at all.

As soon as I entered the Priest's office, I saw four senior members of the house, including the Priest himself, sitting behind a long table. The caretaker, who had stopped me on Friday when Nkanyi came to visit, was there as well. I immediately sensed trouble as the Priest ushered me to a chair. I knew I was here because of those stolen moments of passion with Nkanyi, but everyone on the panel greeted me in a friendly manner as the Priest introduced each of his colleagues to me.

'Mr Njomane, I think you might have by now sensed the reason why you have been called to appear before this committee,' began the Priest, looking at me.

I shook my head. 'No, I have no idea at all.'

'If I may remind you then. On Friday afternoon you took a lady to your room. I don't have to tell you the rules here, you should know them by now.' He paused and took a sip of water from the glass in front of him. 'Mr Njomane, you have been given a verbal warning about your behaviour on two separate occasions, on the 21st of March and also on the 2nd of April, according to my records. Is that not so?' He lifted his eyes from the file in front of him.

'That's true.'

'And you received a suspension?'

'Precisely as the records say in front of you.'

'But yesterday, before you even finished serving your suspension, you bribed James here to let you take a girl up to your room.'

'I didn't bribe anybody.'

'I was actually watching you from the rest-room. I saw you going up to your room with a girl in a floral dress, which as you know is against the rules.'

'That might be so, but I didn't bribe anybody.'

'James here has been suspended for a month because he has admitted his guilt. And that's why we have called you to come and explain yourself,' continued another member of the panel.

'Oh, is that so?' I said uninterestedly.

'I'm afraid so, Mr Njomane. The panel would like to ask you a few questions to make sure that you understand that rules here are not applied arbitrarily. Afterwards we will decide what to do if you are indeed guilty of the offence,' concluded the Priest.

Everything they said sounded like I was on trial. I immediately felt dehydrated.

'May I have a glass of water please?' I asked.

'Help yourself.'

I yawned again as I poured some water into a glass. I didn't make any attempt to cover my mouth. Everybody in the panel turned away in disgust.

'So do you admit having gone with a lady to your room?' asked one of the members of the panel as soon as I had finished drinking my glass of water. He had red whiskers covering his cheeks.

There was a pause. I looked at the ceiling and then at James, who was at that stage twiddling his thumbs on the table. I joined him by crackling my knuckles. The Priest became irritated by our behaviour.

'Will you two stop it!' he snapped at both of us, unable to contain his anger.

I looked at the Priest and felt the anger seething through my veins; I hated being snapped at like that.

'Mr Njomane, we don't have the whole day. Can you please answer the question?'

'What if I don't answer the question?'

'We'll have to assume you are guilty and take the appropriate steps.'

'What if I say I want to talk to my lawyer first?'

'Then we'll tell you that this is not a court of law.'

I knew there was no escape. The Priest and myself had been at loggerheads for quite some time over many issues. He had even called me a reprobate and threatened to chuck me out of his residence at one stage.

'Once more Mr Njomane, did you enter your room with a lady yesterday at about half past three in the afternoon?' asked the Priest in an impatient tone of voice.

'Yes I did.'

'Were you aware that it is against the rules to do so?'

'Absolutely.'

There was a pause as the Priest and his colleagues looked at each other for a while and then nodded. The Priest looked at his file again.

'So having admitted that you did in fact take a lady to your room yesterday, do you now remember bribing James?'

'That's a lie. I never bribed anybody.'

'Interesting,' he continued sarcastically. 'So tell us then. How did you manage to take a lady to your room after talking to James, who is supposed to stop this kind of thing happening?'

'Listen, what I remember is that James told me that it was against the rules to take a lady to my room, but I just ignored him and forced my way past,' I said.

'Would you like to tell us the reason why you did that?'

'Yes.'

'And what was your reason, Mr Njomane?'

All the panel members looked at me, waiting eagerly to hear what I was going to come up with. I felt sick of their strict rules. *If they knew that I first discovered sex when I was twelve they wouldn't treat me like this,* I thought to myself.

Inside that Christian prison I ate whatever they gave me to eat, whenever they said it was time to eat. I slept whenever they said it was time to sleep. I knew that the Priest hated my drinking; there had been many complaints that each time Dworkin and myself came back from the bar during the small hours we woke other students up with the noise we made. I had wanted a reason to be reallocated to another, better residence for a long time now. I had fought with the accommodation office to reallocate me, but they only gave me promises on top of promises.

I didn't have any reason to answer the Priest's question; I knew that they had probably already reached a verdict against me before they even called me in to make my confession.

'You want to know the reason? It's because I'm a healthy young heterosexual male and not a celibate eunuch like other people around here.'

The whole panel scowled in disbelief. I sat there and looked at the Priest who was fidgeting in his chair. His face was flushed with anger caused by my animal-like behaviour. There was a moment of silence. Then another member of the panel with a big stomach who was sitting next to the Priest said:

'What did you just say?'

'Why don't you ask your friends,' I replied.

'You little devil!'

Before I could respond, the Priest, who knew all about my temper, tried to get me to keep a civil tongue in my head.

'Mr Njomane, the purpose of this committee is to maintain order in this house. So if you can at least try to be civilised we would appreciate it, although we realise it might be hard for you,' cautioned the Priest with no little amount of sarcasm.

The implications of the Priest's words left my blood boiling.

'Go to hell! Do you think this place is heaven?'

'Mind your words, boy, when you talk to us.'

'Or what, heh?'

'At this point we are dismissing you from our care. You'll get your dismissal letter this afternoon, ordering you to vacate our premises within five days. Are we clear?' said the pot-bellied member of the panel.

'Fuck that! I don't give a shit.'

'Fine. Go where you think they'll tolerate your unruly behaviour.'

'Arseholes,' I cursed them under my breath as I raised myself from the chair.

As I walked out of the office the members of the panel were still talking amongst themselves. I had heard my verdict; I had made my bed and I had to lie on it. But I knew exactly what I was going to do the following Monday. I would take my dismissal letter to the Accommodation Office so that they would have to re-allocate me. I didn't have any sense of regret whatsoever about my actions.

Reaching my room, I slumped on my bed, hoping to fall asleep again, but sleep would not come easily. I just lay on my bed facing the ceiling and contemplating my situation. I switched on the radio, but I was not in the mood for listening to anything after what had just happened in the Priest's office. I got up again and made my way to the toilet, which was opposite my room. After running some water into the ceramic basin, I plunged both hands into the water and ran it over my face.

I went into the cubicle and lifted the toilet seat up; the toilet still smelt of vomit, as I had thrown up the previous night. I unzipped my trousers for a piss, but instead of pissing peacefully as usual, I felt a strange dull pain coming from my penis and my balls seemed very itchy. I waited for the urine to pass through the duct, but nothing happened. Then, as I tried to force out the hot urine that I felt in my bladder, I felt a terrible twinge and cried out with pain.

After five minutes of struggling to empty my bladder, a trickle of thick yellowish urine came out. I closed my eyes and took a long deep breath in an attempt to hold back the pain that I felt and to stop myself from screaming.

Lunchtime came but I had no appetite. I knew that I had to force something into my stomach since I hadn't had any breakfast. I got up from the bed and picked up my lunchtime meal tickets. I felt weak as I locked my door and before I could go very far I felt the need to piss again. I rushed to the toilet but this time the urine took even longer to come out of my bladder and the pain was even more acute than before.

Deciding against going to the dining-hall for lunch that afternoon, I returned to my bed. Sleep apprehended me forty minutes later and I slept until it was almost time for dinner at around six in the evening. When I woke up a brown envelope had been slipped under my door; it was the dismissal letter from the residence. I had been given until the following Friday to vacate my room.

eighteen

The following Monday at dawn I felt an acute pain. Reaching down I could feel that I had grown a bubo in my groin. I tried to ignore the pain and stared at the ceiling, where two butterflies fluttered around the glowing electric bulb.

My memory revisited the innocent days of my childhood, when we used to chase butterflies around and try to catch them. If we caught one we would rub its powdery wings against our pubic space, as we believed that by doing this we would grow pubic hair. One day after performing this little ritual I carefully plucked out a few hairs from my head, which I stuck onto my pubic space before running to show my friends the power of our butterfly medicine. My friends circled around me to witness the miracle.

The day after I lied to my friends, telling them that I had grown pubic hair, a teenage girl from next door and her friend took me and a certain girl who lived at the far end of our street to an open space by the railway line. I was twelve years old and the girl was fourteen. The two older girls ordered both us to strip naked. It was the girl who took off her clothes first. She already had pubic hair. When it was my turn to strip, I only took off my dirty T-shirt. I was afraid that everybody I had lied to about the magic of the butterfly medicine would see that my pubic space was as hairless as my face.

'Hey! I said take off those shorts before I smack you,' shouted one of the older girls.

'I will do it through the zip,' I answered, unzipping my grubby shorts.

'I said take off all your clothes,' she repeated.

'Please!' I pleaded. 'I will do it better through the zip.'

Seeing that I was stubborn, the two girls held me and undressed me. I didn't have any underwear on. There were giggles all round.

The girl was ordered to lie still on the ground and face the empty sky. Her dirty skinny legs were spread apart and I was shoved naked on top of her. My little uncircumcised penis refused to wake up, but I was afraid to offer any other resistance.

'Is it in?' asked the older girl.

'Ride, boy!' ordered her friend as she pressed my pale buttocks harder against the poor girl.

'Is it in now?' asked the older girl again.

The girl on the ground simply shook her head. One of the older girls jerked me up again. She held my little penis and shook it hard, hoping that I would get an erection. Suddenly two elderly women came past and everybody ran away into the nearby bushes.

A sharp pain from my groin disturbed me from my reminiscence. I knew for sure that I had contracted some kind of STD. I started cursing the day I slept with Nkanyi.

My alarm clock read half past six, but I was too shy to go to the dining-hall for breakfast. I walked with difficulty to the toilet.

Pus, which had run out of my penis, had dried and stuck my penis to my underwear with some blanket fluff. My dark penis had swollen and was for some reason very shiny. I winced with pain as I tried to separate my penis from my underwear; it was as if a needle was being shoved into the duct of my penis. I fell against the wall and covered my face with my hands.

After I had regained my composure I sat carefully on the side of the bath and ran the water so that nobody could hear me. While the water was running, I tried to detach my penis again but the pain was unbearable. I got into the bath and began to soak my penis and the pus that had stuck it to my underwear. Very slowly and carefully I detached it and took off my wet underwear.

Finishing my bath, I decided that I didn't want to experience that pain again. I decided to risk going to the campus wearing only my shorts and a T-shirt, no underwear at all. My plan was to consult the campus doctor as quickly as possible.

As I limped along Jorissen Street to the campus clinic, my swollen penis wagged freely inside my unzipped shorts, where the Monday morning breeze was busy cooling it. My right hand was inside my pocket holding my penis so that it didn't knock against the zip of my shorts.

I always ignored the big billboard at the end of the street, even though I passed it on my way to campus every day. However, that particular Monday it got my attention. There was a red ribbon on it and a hand holding a condom. The inscription read:

DON'T BE SORRY, BE CAREFUL.
AIDS KILLS.
BE WISE AND ALWAYS USE A CONDOM.
DON'T BECOME ANOTHER STATISTIC.

I became very scared. The thought of the HIV and AIDS overwhelmed me as I limped my way towards the clinic.

It took me about thirty minutes to limp the fifteen-minute walk. When I finally reached the clinic, I found that all the morning consultation hours were fully booked. The only available appointment was at half past twelve that afternoon. Unfortunately I had a lecture at that time, but I scrawled my name in the book in the reception anyway.

At quarter past nine my political studies lecture started in number three lecture theatre in the Central Block. I was the first one to arrive; I was ten minutes early. It was the last lecture of the semester before the mid-year exams. I snuggled down on the seat by the wall, third row from the back. I didn't want to be disturbed by latecomers pushing past me to get to the empty seats in the middle of the row, as my shorts were still unzipped to allow fresh air to blow onto my swollen penis. A few students started drifting

140

in for the morning lecture. Theks and Babes came in laughing. They scanned the lecture theatre for a good position and located some empty seats in the second row from the front. They didn't notice me. Then Dworkin arrived. He stood looking for someone he knew for a while, and then noticed me. Smiling a little he walked up the steps to the empty seat next to me. He hadn't slept at our room over the weekend; the last time I had seen him was at the Dropout bar.

Our short, goofy-toothed professor shushed us from the podium, interrupting our conversations. He then put his papers and a tall glass of water on the lectern. He was wearing his trademark worn brown corduroy trousers and his black turtleneck sweater.

'Good morning, class,' he lisped nasally. 'I know that you're still happy from celebrating that you've voted and I share with you the merriment that the ANC has won a memorable victory. But now let's put that behind us and focus on the real issues.' He paused and took a sip from his glass of water. 'The last time we met we finished by talking about the term "politics",' said the professor, carefully putting down his glass of water. 'We'd agreed that the term politics connotes power and that the word power has different meanings: it can be economic power, cultural power, social power and even political power. Unless you have a question concerning that we can move on to our new topic.' He paused and looked at his academic disciples, as Jesus must have done when imparting the Ten Commandments. Then glanced at his papers on the lectern before continuing.

'Great then. Today we move to another interesting topic: democracy. That is topic number four on your handout. I asked you to look at the topic in your course reader over the weekend and I guess you all did.' He paused and looked from one student to another while searching for an answer. 'How many of you managed to do that?'

I hadn't bothered to study that weekend. There was no reason why I should copy the others and lie to the professor by raising my hand. Why should I study democracy anyway? I already knew what it meant; I thought everybody knew the term. Even my mother knew what it meant, although she didn't have any formal education and didn't even speak English, and only experienced the reality of it the day she voted for the first time at the age of seventy-one.

There was no way that I would waste my time reading about that tired, misused term.

Professor McGregor looked pleased to see a considerable number of raised hands from his students. He smiled and nodded with approval, as if this was a rare, pleasing sight from his not-so-educated students. Even Dworkin and Theks had raised their hands with great aplomb, but I doubted if Dwork knew what he was doing. The professor looked around before his eyes landed on a black female student who was sitting behind Theks.

'Yes. Can you please define the term democracy for us?' asked the professor, pointing at the female student.

The rest of the students put their hands down and waited for the lady to speak. I was thinking about what I'd heard from some of my second-year friends, who had told me of a subtle form of racism practised by some white lecturers. My sources had explained that these white lecturers didn't know their black students by name, and that was why they often said 'yes' when asking them to respond to a question. As for the white students, the white professors always addressed them politely by their full names.

I listened as the girl began to speak with her plastic Anglophile accent.

'The term democracy refers to a government by the people as a whole rather than by any section, class or interest within it,' she said.

She had said pretty much what I would have said myself. The professor was nodding his head in approval. There was a pause as he brushed his hair back from his face with his hand.

'Any objections or additions to that definition?' asked the professor, pushing his thick-lensed glasses back into the desired position.

'OK then, my definition seems to differ from hers,' began the professor, while everybody else prepared to take notes. 'To me democracy is a logical response to paranoia: a diplomatic and ideological phantasm invented by the bourgeoisie, or the property-owning class, to safeguard their property interests; or, if you're a Marxist, their relation with production, when feeling threatened by the masses. In the process the bourgeoisie create a false consciousness to . . .' he paused as he saw hands flying from all angles.

The professor took off his lenses and put them on the lectern next to his glass of water. He rubbed his bloodshot eyes with his fat index finger and started looking around to pick a student with a raised hand.

I felt a twinge from my groin again. My penis had accidentally wagged against the zip of my shorts while I was scrawling those sophisticated words of wisdom from the learned professor. I flinched and immediately stopped scribbling. The professor put his glasses back on and pointed at a tall white student.

'Mr Rutherford,' he said.

'Can you please speak in English, sir,' the student pleaded.

There was laughter from all around the lecture theatre. We laughed at the paradox of Mr Rutherford's words – he sounded very English himself.

The professor seemed not to have taken any offence and sipped his glass of water while the students continued laughing and talking. I only managed to snigger, because of the pain. Mr Rutherford was right: I'd thought that my inability to understand what the professor was saying was because English was my second language, but the problem was with the professor himself, who was enjoying hiding the meaning of what he was actually saying.

The pain continued. I looked around to see if anybody was looking at me. The white girl immediately behind me was already snoozing. I wondered if she had had a mixed-up weekend like mine. Another white female student in the fourth row shushed the class as the professor started to respond.

'All right then. I'll try to give an illustration of what I'm saying.' He paused and looked at his lecture notes again. 'When you voted on the 27th of April, you were convinced that you were voting for democracy. Elections and universal suffrage are now seen as essential features of democracy, but they may be undemocratic at the same time. For example, every constitution requires a framework of offices and conventions that will not be subject to easy amendments by popular choice or *vox populi*. Moreover, a democratically elected government may proceed to enact, during its term of office, policies that are manifestly in conflict with the wishes and interests of the people.' He paused and scanned his academic disciples to see if we were all still on the same page. 'Therefore the question we have to ask ourselves is: is democracy just another form of perceived freedom or is it truly the ability to realise oneself in autonomous choices? Think about that for next week's lecture, ladies and gentlemen,' concluded the professor.

Before the professor could pack away his papers and books, another hand was raised by a black male student, pleading with him to speak louder. I was at that stage feeling a bit drowsy; I had used too much energy scrawling down the professor's words and nursing my ailment. I could feel that I was running on low on reserves. Packing away his papers, the professor responded apathetically: 'Don't just scribble down everything that I say. It would be helpful if you listened in future.'

'But Prof . . . I mean . . .'

'Come with me to my office if you want to know something in particular,' snapped the professor.

There was some mild laughter that woke up the girl who had been snoozing behind me. It was ten o'clock already. The lecture was over and the students were preparing to go. As the white girl behind me leaned forward in an attempt to put away her pa-

144

pers, she spilled her already cold coffee down my back. I felt it flow uncomfortably into my arse crack. Some drops of it landed on my swollen penis through my zip that was still undone. Dworkin scowled as he assessed his coffee-stained yellow T-shirt. I looked at the girl, but only managed a pathetic sneer.

Pleading apologetically, the girl looked at us until we feigned some apology-accepted nods. Showing some partial relief, she walked down the steps and left with Mr Rutherford, who had been waiting for her by the exit.

Within seconds, Dwork's anger turned into a smile. I squirmed with embarrassment.

'Joe your nkauza is out,' said Dworkin, his hand over his mouth to stifle his amusement.

'Uhh. Thanks. I didn't see,' I said.

'You lie?'

'I'm not lying.'

'I've already seen, man. Just tell me what happened.'

'Ag man. It's my weekend thing. I have a bubo.'

'A bubo on the nkauza?' he asked in disbelief as we descended to the lectern, where Theks was waiting for us. Babes had already rushed to the West Campus to attend a sociology lecture.

Theks also noticed my limp as I descended the steps.

'Hi guys. What happened to your leg?' she asked, not even giving the two of us a chance to respond to her greeting.

'It's a minor bubo on my groin,' I answered.

'Hmm,' she hemmed sceptically. 'I thought I would see you at home over the weekend; where were you?'

'Well, I didn't manage it. Something came up.'

'You! We'll see,' she said accusingly.

'What?'

Without answering me she turned to Dworkin. 'Oh jeez, what happened to your T-shirt?'

'That racist white lady spilled her coffee on us.'

'It was just a mistake, man,' I corrected him.

145

'You don't know white people, man. It was on purpose,' he insisted.

'What would she gain by doing that?'

'Wake up, man. They just want to show you that they are still in charge after they were embarrassed when the ANC won the elections.'

'You talk shit!'

'Uhh, my gosh! Dwork, we'll be late for the tutorial. C'mon, let's go,' said Theks, pulling Dwork after her down the corridor.

'Ay sani, I forgot about that,' replied Dwork.

'See you in class at twelve, Dingz,' shouted Theks. 'Adios!'

I wasn't going to come to that lecture at twelve. As soon as they had disappeared around the corner I limped to the toilet to assess the damage. Entering the toilet I envied the guys who were standing on the platform pointing their healthy dicks at the urinal. Agitated, I scanned the doors; the toilets were all occupied. I went to the basins and ran some cold water into one of them, soaked my hands and scrubbed my face with both hands. The mirror reflected my unhappy face.

After a few minutes a guy came out of one of the toilets. I could feel that my bladder was full of hot urine. I closed the door quickly behind me and took down my pants. My swollen penis was stuck to my left thigh with pus, but it wasn't difficult to detach it this time, as the pus hadn't had time to dry. I tried to urinate, but as before nothing came out. I tried to force it. The pain was unbearable.

Defeated, I sat on the toilet. A lot of junk had been written on the formerly white walls. Some graffiti caught my interest and I hunched forward to read it.

KAFFIRS INVADED OUR FATHERLAND, VIVA AWB

ONE SETTLER ONE BULLET – VIVA AZANIA

THIS COUNTRY BELONGS TO BLACKS, FUCK ALL THE WHITES

WHITES MUST START TO LIVE IN THE CONDITIONS STIPULATED BY BLACKS OR MUST LEAVE THE COUNTRY PEACEFULLY

After five minutes brooding on the toilet some hot urine came out at last. I covered my mouth with my hand to prevent myself from squeaking with pain. I was afraid that people might think that I was masturbating in the toilet.

nineteen

It was about half past eleven when I arrived at the accommodation office. There were five guys sitting on the bench outside, waiting to be helped. After twenty minutes it was my turn and the student assistant called me inside.

'It's you again,' said Mrs Keller, the residence co-ordinator.

She flashed her coffee-stained teeth in a welcoming smile as I entered her office. She sighed, pretending that she was fed-up with my familiar face, then forced out another little smile.

'So what can I do for you today?'

'I need a place to stay very urgently,' I replied.

'What's wrong with your present res?'

'The Priest chucked me out yesterday,' I said, showing her my letter of dismissal.

Mrs Keller read my dismissal letter and leant backwards in her maroon swivel chair.

'How did this happen?'

'I was caught with a girl inside my room.'

She laughed. 'Come on now, be serious.'

'I am serious.'

'Ha, ha. Just like that?'

'Yes. No ladies are allowed to enter our rooms.'

'So . . . so why did you do it if you knew that it was against the rules?' she asked, pulling her chair closer to the desk.

'For academic purposes.'

'Ha! What do you mean?'

'We were discussing the political studies essay that is due this Friday.'

'Liar. What's the name of the lady?' she asked.

'I'm serious. Her name is Thekwini Mkwanazi.'

'Are you sure?'

'Absolutely.'

'Yhaa! What's your student number?'

'940661Y.'

Mrs Keller stood up and waddled toward her shelves, which were mounted on the white walls of her office. She picked out one green file with *1994 YMCA RESIDENCE* written on the front, opened it and carried it over to the table. After a few minutes she took a pink highlighter and highlighted something on a page inside the file. She looked at me and punched my student number into her computer, shaking her head.

'We have just received an e-mail from the Y, from Minister Smith. He says you insulted a panel of ministers during a meeting. He also says that you have admitted that you were guilty of bringing ladies into the residence and that most weekends you come back to the residence drunk and wake the other students in the early hours of the morning. You play your music too loud and you are very rude to the cleaning ladies. Ja, I think they don't want you anymore.'

'Is that so?'

'I'm afraid so.'

'So, put me in another res.'

'Well, you see Mr Njomane, we'll have to put you on our waiting list.'

'But where will I stay in the meantime?'

'Where do you live? I mean, where is your home?'

'Soweto.'

'I'm afraid all our residences are full at the moment. And since you're originally from Soweto it will be difficult for us to process your application quickly. I mean, there are students here who come from as far as the Eastern Cape and Northern Province and have no place to stay. You live just here in Soweto – I'm sure you won't have too much trouble travelling every day,' concluded Mrs Keller.

'But Mrs Keller, as I mentioned when I was first applying for the res, my mother is a pensioner and my home is not conducive to studying because I still sleep in the sitting-dining-room and both my neighbours run shebeens.'

'I know that. But remember we did you a great favour letting you stay at the res in the first place. We're supposed to give preference to those who come from far away. Besides, you're the one who blew your chance. As I said, I will put your name on the waiting list. Maybe if you're lucky next month something might come up.'

'Oh, my gosh. This happened just at the wrong time when the exams are at the door,' I whispered to myself.

'Yeah, well, you should have thought about that before you fell out with the Priest.'

That was it, the end of my cheese life at the Y. Back to square one. I was to travel every day from home to the campus. I limped out of Mrs Keller's office with bitterness in my heart. I was going back to the ghetto's unbalanced diet. *Why is this happening to me?* I asked myself.

As I passed the main library on the East Campus lawns my eye was drawn to a white caravan that was parked there. A big red and white sign caught my eye:

DONATE BLOOD AND SAVE LIVES.

Some students were sitting on plastic chairs next to the caravan. They were there to donate their blood. *Is mine clean, or do I already have AIDS?* I wondered as I limped down the stairs towards the campus clinic. A tall white lady who had been standing by the caravan flashed her teeth in a fake smile and gave me a flier. I took it and continued with my journey. Without looking at the paper I threw it into the bin by the door of the clinic.

It was quarter past twelve by the time I finally got to the clinic. Just as I arrived a student, clutching a box of free condoms, came out with his eyes hidden beneath layers of pain. There were also a few students seated on the waiting-room bench opposite the reception area. Most of them looked absorbed in reading the old magazines piled on the table. I sat on the bench as well and waded through an old copy of *Time* magazine.

Within ten minutes a white female doctor in her late forties called me into the consultation room. She was wearing a white coat and had thick-lensed glasses. I put the magazine down and followed her to a room that had 'Dr Hewson' written on the door. The doctor was very polite and made me feel at home; after introducing herself she began asking me her doctor-patient questions.

'So what's troubling you, my dear?' she asked.

'My private part is not functioning well.'

'What is wrong exactly?'

'When I go to the loo to urinate I feel some pain and only sticky, yellowish urine comes out of my system.'

'Mmm. I see. When did this start to happen?'

'The day before yesterday.'

'Is that the only thing troubling you?'

'I also have a painful bubo.'

'Where?'

'Well . . . eh . . . well,' I stammered a bit. 'Well on my groin, and here,' I pointed at my arse.

Doctor Hewson got up from her chair and walked slowly towards a cupboard by the wall. She took out a pair of transparent latex gloves and put them on. Then she took a beaker and handed it to me. I writhed in embarrassment as she asked me to go into a small room that looked like a fitting-room in a clothing store and pee into the beaker for her.

I closed the curtain behind me, closed my eyes and pulled out all the stops to force some urine out of my bladder. It took me about five minutes to fill only half the beaker. As soon as I came out she began talking.

'Don't be afraid of your own urine. I treat almost a hundred students each week with this type of sickness,' she said as she took the urine from me.

She sat on her chair, put my urine on her desk and began to examine it with a magnifying glass. She went back to her cupboard with it and poured something else into the beaker, but I couldn't see what she was doing as she had her back to me. After about five minutes she drew away from the cupboard and, looking at me inquisitively, came back to the table.

'What you are suffering from is an STD called gonorrhoea; ever heard of it?'

'Yes . . . Oh my gosh!'

'Next time you must quickly consult a doctor as soon as you start feeling any pain.'

'Is it very bad?'

'You are lucky because it is still in its early stages. If you had waited before you came to see me it could have developed into something more complicated.'

'Oh. Thank God!' I closed my eyes with my hands.

'Does your girlfriend know about this?'

'I don't think so.'

'Is she a student too?'

'Yes, but not at this campus.'

'OK then. Contact her today and tell her to consult a doctor as soon as possible.'

'I will.'

She ushered me to a single bed next to her table and asked me to take off my T-shirt. She put a thermometer under my tongue to check my body temperature. Then she held her stethoscope against my ribs and listened to my chest.

'OK, get off the bed and pull your shorts down,' she ordered, removing the thermometer.

'What?' I asked, as if I didn't understand.

'Off the bed and pull them down.'

I squirmed.

'The purpose is not to embarrass you. But I need to make sure that gonorrhoea is the only disease that you have. You said you have a bubo down there, is that not so?' she asked.

'Yes.'

'You see? Now bend over!'

I pulled my shorts down and bent over. She stuck her finger deep into my arse. I felt very embarrassed and the pain from the bubo was unbearable.

'Are you allergic to injections?'

'Well, I don't know.'

'OK then.'

She went over to her desk and took out a needle. She came over to me and injected the side of my penis. I grunted, not because I felt pain, but simply at the sight of the needle.

'You can get dressed now,' she instructed, going to her desk. 'Come over here when you're done.'

As I limped back into the changing room I noticed a dildo wearing a condom at the far end of her table. Next to it was a pile of small white boxes with condoms inside.

When I came out of the changing room she was at her desk, scrawling something in a file. Opening the bottom drawer in her desk, she came up with two packets of pills; some large multi-coloured pills and some smaller greenish pills.

'Take one of each three times a day.'

'All right.'

'Please come back to me if you still don't feel any better by Thursday.'

'I will,' I said, taking the pills.

'Before I forget, here is something for you.' She gave me one of the boxes of condoms. 'Remember, it's your life that you are risking.'

'No, ehh . . .' I stammered. 'I promise I do use them. It's just a condom which broke in the middle of . . . you know.'

'So you felt it and then continued, hey?' she asked, smiling.

'No. I only felt it when the damage was already done.'

'Whether that's true or not, you're only fooling yourself.'

'It's true.'

'How old are you?'

'Nineteen.'

'You still have a great future ahead of you, so please don't muck it up.'

'Yes ma'am,' I replied, smiling.

'And you must also consider taking a blood test to find out whether you have contracted anything else.'

'I'll think about that,' I said as I stood up.

'Promise I won't see you again here with the same type of sickness?'

'I promise,' I said, clutching my boxes of pills.

In the corridor I stopped and looked at the file that she had also given me. From her ugly writing I could only read:

Urethral discharge – Yellow. Prescription – Use condom.

By half past three I was back at the Y; the injection had performed a little miracle: the pain had disappeared and I could manage to walk normally again.

I received a call while I was busy packing up some of my stuff. It was Nkanyi and she sounded very worried.

'What happened to you over the weekend?' she asked.

'I fell ill, and that is why I didn't call you.'

'Why do you sound so cold, like you do not appreciate my call?'

'Oh no. You know that your voice is the nicest thing I would like to hear. It's just that my weekend was nuts since you left.'

'What happened?'

'I had a serious squabble with the Priest and I have been dismissed from the res.'

'Why didn't you tell me instead of keeping me waiting for you all day? I have been trying to call you all morning.'

'I'm sorry. I just didn't want to spoil your weekend with my bad mood. But I promise I will make it up to you.'

'We'll see about that.'

'Look Nkanyi, I will be moving out of the res this coming Friday.'

'Oh, I see.'

'Aren't you happy that we'll be travelling together by train?'

'Yeah, that's nice.'

'So, we'll be seeing each other almost every day.'

'Yes. But if I didn't call you when would I have heard this?'

'I meant to call you tonight as we have to talk about something more serious.'

'What?'

'Something we can't discuss over the phone, but you'll have to come by today or tomorrow.'

'I can't manage today. I insist you tell me what's so serious.'

'OK then, if you insist. I was diagnosed with gonorrhoea today and the doctor said I should tell you to consult a doctor as well, before it turns into something more complicated.'

I was happy that had I finally summoned up the courage to tell her. There was a silence on the other end of the line.

'I was also feeling a bit sick over the weekend. I was worried that you never even bothered to call me to find out how I was.'

'I'm very sorry to hear that. How are you feeling now?'

'A lot better; I even managed to wake up and go to campus.'

'That's good, but promise me you'll go to a doctor today.'

'I'll try.'

'Don't try, just do it.'

'OK. I promise I'll go.'

'I'll call you after seven at home tonight.'

'Make it half past eight because I'll still be watching *The Bold* and *Generations*.'

'All right. Bye for now. And still love you.'

'Me too. Bye.'

155

twenty

On a Friday afternoon in the last week of June I sat on the grey steps outside the Great Hall. The weak winter sun had failed to break through the scattered cloud. I had been basking in the patchy sunlight for about forty minutes contemplating what my next step should be. I knew that I had my work cut out. Things had not gone according to plan.

It had all started the week before when I had gone to the exam room badly prepared. I had written another paper the day before and hadn't had time to prepare for this one as well.

After I was handed the question paper by the invigilator, I found that most of the things on it were new to me. At that point everything became confusing and I decided to slip out of the exam room without being noticed. I was not going to embarrass myself by writing a paper I knew I wasn't fully prepared for.

After sneaking out of the exam room, I went straight to the clinic and feigned a blackout. All that I wanted was a valid reason for absconding. After the examination, which didn't even take five minutes, Doctor Hewson gave me her diagnosis.

'I can't see anything wrong with you,' she said, smiling. 'Maybe you're a hypochondriac.'

I shrugged my shoulders. 'But I just saw black today. My eyes were very painful and I had a serious headache.'

'Did you get enough sleep last night or in the days before that?'

'Well, I guess I didn't get my normal sleep. I was preparing for my exams.'

'That could be the problem. Sleep is very important for the body to rest and prepare for another day.'

'Oh, I see.'

'I would also advise you to avoid eating fish or chicken during the time of an exam. They can contribute to sleeplessness because they contain tyrosine, which is an amino acid that can increase alertness.'

I was very disappointed with Doctor Hewson's diagnosis. I had expected something more than the letter she had scrawled for me, in which she simply confirmed that I had consulted her immediately after suffering from my so-called blackout. I tried several times to convince her of my situation and although she had sounded very sympathetic, she insisted that there was nothing more she could do, as it would be against the ethics of her profession. When I took her scanty letter to the professor he had refused to grant me an aegrotat, arguing that there was insufficient reason.

On the following day I submitted the letter to the dean of the faculty. I was hoping that if I piled on the agony I could convince him to overrule his colleague. The dean took a brief look at the letter and shoved it away disapprovingly.

'I'm sorry, there's no reason to grant you an aegrotat,' said the dean in his soft Irish accent, shaking his head, 'and unless you come up with something more serious we'll have no option but to mark you absent.'

'But Prof, I was seriously ill on that day,' I insisted.

'Going to the clinic doesn't necessarily mean that a person is ill,' said the dean. 'What you had on the day of the exam was a mere temporary blackout and that isn't covered in the rules and regulations for granting an aegrotat.'

'But Prof, surely you can make an exception?'

'You're trying your luck, aren't you?' he asked with a mock smile. 'If I made an exception for you I'd be opening the floodgates for all the other students who've absconded from their exams without a proper reason,' he said loud and clear. 'As I've already told you, without a convincing letter there's actually nothing I can do but to mark you absent.'

I was left with no choice but to start fabricating a story. I didn't want to fail the exam because of the lousy reason of being marked absent.

'I understand Prof, but my blackout was a result of the shock news that I received about the death of my cousin. You know I was very close with the deceased,' I lied.

I faked a grieved expression, searching his eyes for sympathy.

Silence simmered for a short while between the dean and myself. He started twiddling his thick thumbs. I tried to maintain eye contact, but he looked away and began to scan the table as if something had just gone missing.

'I'm sorry about the misfortune that has befallen your family. But you'll need to submit the death certificate according to our procedure.'

'So when will you need the certificate?'

'Next Friday,' he said. 'That's the last date for an aegrotat hearing.'

'Is it possible to extend that deadline for me? It would be very difficult at this point in time for me to ask for the death certificate at home. According to my culture, the deceased's property is regarded as sacred for about a month after the burial.'

'I'm sorry, then. That's all we can do for you.'

'But Prof, there should be some leeway in a case like this.'

'As I said, I'm afraid those are the rules.'

'All right then. I'll try to ask for it.'

'Great, now let me see you out,' said the dean, ushering me out of his office.

When I left the dean's office that Friday morning I went straight to the Great Hall piazza to mull over our conversation. I realised that I had jumped in at the deep end. Nevertheless, I told myself that where there is a will there is always a way.

Meanwhile I had learnt from Theks that Paul and Nikki, my white friends, didn't sit the exam either. However, they had been granted deferred exams because they had consulted their family doctors for medical certificates. Nikki was the tall strawberry blonde who had spilt coffee down my back during the political studies lecture. You only had to look at her to conclude that she was born with a silver spoon in her mouth. She was a paragon of blonde beauty, with her heartbreakingly slender body and her teeth arranged like maize on the cob.

A couple of weeks earlier she had taken us all, Dwork, Theks and myself, for a snack at the Senate House cafeteria. Dwork and myself thought she was doing that just to show how sorry she was for spilling her coffee on us. Nikki had paid for all of us, including Paul Rutherford, her tall white friend. As she bought the jam doughnuts, muffins, chelsea buns, cooldrinks and juices, I enviously glanced at the banknotes in her purse. They were spread like confetti. After that, seeing her always reminded me of my cashless campus life.

I had become close to Nikki. Dwork had encouraged me to make a move on her, and although I had great mind to do so, I remained chicken-hearted; I was afraid that she would spurn my advances and call them sexual harassment.

Meanwhile Paul and Theks had also become close. It was easy to tell that he had the hots for her by the way he acted when the two of them were together, and we could see that their friendship was developing into something else. Our minds grimed with jealousy, Dwork and myself felt that Theks was getting assimilated into Paul's Anglophone tribe. He even managed to convince me that Theks was considering changing her surname from Mkwanazi to McNizze so that it sounded more English. I wouldn't have been suprised, as she had responded happily when Paul and his friends began calling her Tequila instead of Thekwini. Dwork was so concerned about Theks that he accused her of enjoying her white friends' company more than ours.

Theks's five-year relationship with Dunga was on the rocks. This we attributed to the beginning of a romance with Paul. She had even written Dunga an e-mail the week before, terminating their relationship. The news had devastated Dunga; he had recently confided in me that he was planning to marry Theks as soon as she graduated.

What worried him most was that he had played a major role in her education, giving her both his uncompromising moral and financial support. He couldn't swallow the fact that she had turned against him after everything. In order to bring Dunga to his senses I had promised to pay him a visit that Friday in his office downtown.

I had called Dunga immediately after talking to the dean and told him about my aegrotat problem. He had promised to help me, and told me about the case that he was busy working on at the Johannesburg Magistrates' Court. It concerned a certain Orlando East undertaker who had been being accused of mutilating the penises of corpses and selling them to traditional healers. Dunga was sitting as one of the assessors in that court case. He promised to hook me up with the accused to see if there was anyone with a Njomane surname in his mortuary. We were prepared to buy, borrow or forge a death certificate to get my aegrotat.

I was still basking in the weak winter sun and musing upon my problem on the steps of the piazza when I felt a soft hand on my back. It was Theks (Tequila as she preferred to be called at that stage), Paul, Bob and Nikki. They had come from the main library. Under her left arm, which was as white as uncooked chicken, Nikki was holding a little dog. She was busy showering that little dog with endearments. They all knew that I had not written the exam and that my aegrotat was still pending.

'Hey, why are you sitting all alone? What's on your mind?' It was Nikki, who sat down next to me.

'You don't want to know,' I replied sullenly.

'Shame! Don't you worry,' she said, as she gently rubbed my back.

'I still can't get an aegrotat.'

'Ag man, it will be all right. Now, put on a happy face and have a cigarette,' she said, offering me a Camel.

All of us, including Theks, took a cigarette from her packet.

'What's her name?' I asked Nikki, the lit cigarette between my fingers. Surreptitiously, I looked between the dog's hind legs to make sure that it was female.

'She's Tarbo. Isn't she a beauty?' she said, brushing the little pooch's head.

I burst out laughing. 'You must be the great fan of our Vice President Thabo Mbeki to give your dog his first name.'

Everyone began to laugh, including Nikki. Theks laughed until her eyes were filled with tears. I still didn't get the joke.

'Not Thabo, you idiot,' corrected Nikki playfully while everybody else was still laughing. 'She's Tar-bo, spelled T-A-R.'

'Oh, I see! And what does that mean?'

'Actually my dad called her that because of the shape of her head. It looks as if she is wearing a tarboosh,' she continued, stroking her pooch. 'Isn't she a doll?'

As if the pooch understood those endearments, she licked Nikki's left cheek with her little tongue. *Ag sis, that's disgusting*, I thought. But I forced myself to say something nice.

'She's beautiful.'

'Do you want to hold her? She's very friendly, you know.'

'Yebo, yes I would love to.'

Nikki dropped the dog in my arms. She unzipped her schoolbag and put her packet of Camel cigarettes inside.

I was not a great fan of dogs. All my life I had regarded them as instruments of terror and associated them with acts of brutality. The police often used dogs to brutalise black people during apartheid. Dogs were to me hated creatures that always shat on our lawn, creatures that sneaked to our dustbin in the still of the night and threw disgusting rubbish out all over the street while searching for bones. I also hated their eyes, which glow in the dark, because I associated them with witchcraft, but on that day with Nikki, I wanted to hold Tarbo to impress her. The little dog looked harmless enough. I had to give her the benefit of the doubt; surely the poor pooch knew nothing about apartheid and the township.

'So, why don't you consult your family doctor for a medical certificate?' asked Nikki, lighting a cigarette.

'We don't have a family doctor,' I answered brusquely.

I was annoyed. I wanted to tell her that our family doctor was a traditional healer who did not issue such certificates, and even if he did it would not convince the varsity's white dean. *Ignorance is one of the embarrassing penalties of being rich*, I told myself.

'I'm sorry about that.'

'That's OK. So tell me, why didn't you write the exam?'

Suddenly Tarbo leapt out of my hands, limped down one step and started urinating. Inside I was cursing: *fuck, I hate that creature*.

'I was mad that weekend before the exam,' she said, pretending to scowl.

'What happened?'

'My little Tarbo was hit by a car when we were going walkies to the Cresta shopping mall.' She paused and looked at me. 'I was ve-ry ma-d. You know Tarbo and me have been together for the past five years.'

'Uhh, it was terrible. You know Nikki called me while she was laying a charge at the police station against the driver,' added Paul with a grimace, as if I was the reckless driver he was talking about. 'We took the poor pooch to the vet there by Cresta. I'm telling you Dingz, Tarbo was very scared and confused. You know, I just can't understand how a human being can do such a cruel thing,' he said, slowly shaking his head.

'If it wasn't for Paul, who was there for me throughout that ordeal, I just don't know how I would have coped. I didn't eat the whole day and I had to stay at the vet for more than seven hours, hoping that she'd be OK. I was really m-aadd.'

Theks ran her hand across Nikki's shoulders to comfort her. 'Shame,' she said.

'It's OK. Thanks to Paul who sacrificed his exams for my Tarbo. She won't forget you as well,' she said, craning her long neck beyond me to look at Paul.

'You're more than welcome. That's what friends are for.'

There was a pause. 'You know I bought this doll in Australia when she was only two weeks old. Since then our bond has been unbreakable,' said Nikki.

'And how is she now?' asked Theks, showing a lot of sympathy.

'She is still in the process of recovering. Can you see she limps when she walks?'

'I'm sorry to hear that,' I said, feigning some concern.

'Tell her that I want to see her in good shape when I come for dinner next week after the exams,' said Theks.

'I will. You know she has received more than twenty get well cards from my friends and Dad's staff.'

I was bored with talking about the dog. When I looked at Nikki I saw a frivolous, idle, over-indulged brat. The stylish yellow hat and classy peach dress she was wearing reminded me that she was suffering from affluenza. She chuckled and started playing with a bunch of upmarket car keys. She always said she only enjoyed driving on Fridays, when she went out to gigs. I managed to hide my smouldering anger and excused myself from that bumbling company, as it was time to go and see Dunga.

'See you people, there's somebody I'm meeting downtown,' I said as I prepared to leave.

'Hmm, you have a date, I can tell,' said Nikki, feigning jealousy.

'No. It's just a friend of mine.'

'Somebody you can introduce us to soon?'

'Oh yes. His name is Dunga.'

I looked at Theks to see her reaction. She stared at the floor.

'Would you like to accompany me, Tequila?' I asked sarcastically.

I looked at Paul; his face had suddenly turned white with revulsion. I pretended I didn't notice Theks stroking Paul's back gently to appease him as he tried to hide his anger from me. She blushed.

'I'm sorry, I can't. I'll have to finish reading some chapters in the library. Say hi to him for me.'

'Sure I will.' I turned to the others: 'How about you guys?'

'Same thing as Tequila. But I would love to walk downtown sometime. I've never been there,' said Nikki.

'Huh, that makes both of us. I last went downtown when I was a toddler with my dad,' said Bob.

I left Nikki, Bob, Theks and Paul sitting and smoking cigarettes on the grey steps of the Great Hall as I made my way downtown. I had to procure a death certificate, no matter what.

As I walked the streets to Jo'burg city centre alone I missed the company of Theks, who would usually have accompanied me. I passed a group of homeless kids who were busy playing happily next to the cardboard city they had built under Johann Rissik Bridge. One of them noticed me and immediately withdrew from the group, raising his hand to ask for money. I stopped and looked at him as he gestured to his stomach. He was dirty and his eyes were still full of sleep. Big-heartedly, I searched for a fifty-cent coin in my pocket and tossed it to him. I could see the disapproval on his face immediately.

'Ag sis, what do you think I will buy with fifty cents nowadays?' he whined, unmoved by my kindness.

'Well, if you don't want it I'll take it back,' I said, looking around to locate where the coin had fallen.

After a few seconds I gave up searching for the coin. The other homeless kids were drawing closer, asking their friend what was happening. I felt insulted: he was the one who had asked for my help. I overheard one of them saying they should leave me alone because every time I passed by I always ignored them, and that one of these days I would be sorry. Another kid with dirty hair was carrying an empty juice carton and inhaling something from it – I guess it was glue or benzene. I decided to ignore the homeless kids and went on with my journey; but looking back quickly I saw them searching through the grass for that fifty-cent coin.

twenty-one

I walked through Park Station, which was filled with commuters milling about lazily. Some people were queuing at the kiosks to buy tickets for the trains and buses; others were crowded around the bistros that operate there, buying food and magazines. It was difficult to walk along the concourse because of all the activity, so I decided to rejoin Rissik Street via the long-distance bus terminus. As I was about to do this I saw a large motley crowd in a happy mood: they were dancing and singing as they moved along the street in the direction of Braamfontein.

The crowd was predominantly made up of white people, many of them awkwardly dressed guys wearing mascara and loose robes and sporting curly, peroxide blonde hair. Some of them were wearing hotpants and hosiery and had pierced noses, tongues and ears. Their hair and beards were dyed all sorts of colours and I could also see some with snake-weave haircuts. Those at the front were waving flashing dildos and blowing up condoms like balloons.

I saw them approach the corner of Bree and Rissik Street, chanting loudly and waving banners.

RECOGNIZE GAY AND LESBIAN RIGHTS NOW

**GAYS AND LESBIANS BY NATURE
NOT BY CHOICE**

**STOP TREATING US LIKE EVIL PEOPLE,
WE ARE AS HUMAN AS YOU ARE**

I waited on the pavement for the crowd to pass. A group of unconcerned citizens were clogging the pavement, cheering, whistling and clapping. However the street vendors, who felt that their business sites were being unnecessarily invaded, stood holding as much of their merchandise as they could carry in their arms, sneering impatiently as the marchers passed. Some groups who felt that the march was distasteful also stood on the pavement with counter-banners:

GOD CREATED ADAM AND EVE –
NOT ADAM & ADAM OR EVE & EVE

GOD DOES NOT TOLERATE MORAL SINNERS

GOD CREATED SEX FOR A
MAN AND A WOMAN TO ENJOY

As soon as the crowd had passed I continued my journey to Dunga's office, which was situated at the corner of Rissik and Market Street. I took the lift to the second floor and walked through the glass door that was already open, then across the greyish carpet. I ignored some of Dunga's nosy colleagues who started craning their necks and went straight to his cubicle. Dunga was busy strumming the keyboard of his computer.

I sat down on an empty chair.

'You should have told me before you lied about your cousin's death to the dean. I've got friends who could have made a convincing sblivana without any problem,' said Dunga, a knowing grin pasted on his thick lips.

'Eish, mfowethu, there was no time to think,' I replied, disappointed.

'But broer, you know full well that Themba's grandmother used to be a Bara Hospital nurse. She still has access to the hospital papers. She only charges two tiger for sblivana mzala, and you could have got that within two hours. In fact, she would have gone to the hospital and asked some of the doctors she knows to write something for you.'

'Iyooo!' I said disapprovingly. 'Remember last time Theks's brother lost his job because of her sblivana? When his company called to verify his sickness with the doctor concerned, they found that the telephone number belonged to her shebeen! Her sblivana is suspicious, man.'

'No, man.' Dunga shook his head. 'You know what the problem was? Themba's granny had asked him what disease he wanted her to write on the letter. He told her to write chicken pox – but he'd forgotten that a fortnight earlier he had cited the same disease on his sblivana. His boss became suspicious because no one can have chicken pox twice, so he called the number on the letter. Unfortunately the phone was answered by Themba's baby sister, who confirmed that the place was a shebeen.'

'Oh shit,' I said, laughing. 'But the same thing could have happened to me.'

Slowly, Dunga shook his head. 'Don't you know by now, mfowethu, that risk is two-fold. On one hand there is the possibility of losing, but on the other hand risk is an opportunity itself. Nothing ventured, nothing gained, my friend. Nearly everything in life is a gamble, including your own existence at Wits. If you look for certainties, you have far to reach and little to find in this world; our very existence is uncertainty itself. So it's not a question of the sblivana working or not working, it is a question of how to make that sblivana work for you. If you adopt this attitude it will force you to think and find ways of getting the aegrotat, mfowethu,' he concluded.

'Yeah, I hear you, mfowethu.' I nodded my approval of his philosophy.

'Don't you know that the only language that whites understand in this country is lies. You haven't read *Africa My Music* by Professor Mphahlele? He says exactly what I am saying; that you

167

must lie to the whites in order to survive in this country because the whites themselves already live in the web of a big lie. It's the only thing they understand. So, Theks's brother was just an unfortunate example. He failed to defend his lies properly and that should not discourage you, mfowethu.'

'Oho, I see.'

'But don't you worry, mfowethu. I have already organised everything with Mr Skhosana, the undertaker from Orlando East, and we'll go to the mortuary together tomorrow morning. He said he was too busy to go through the documents himself, but he'll call me at home tonight if he has found anything.'

As Dunga mentioned the mortuary I could suddenly smell death. I imagined entering the morgue where the dead people are kept before burial. I cursed myself for lying to the dean; I wasn't ready to see the tags hanging from the toes of the frozen corpses.

A few minutes later I excused myself from Dunga and went to the toilet next to the lifts to answer a call of nature. There was nobody inside and I chose the middle cubicle. After I had been inside for a couple of minutes I heard the voices of two people coming into the toilet; one of them went into the first cubicle, the other one stood on the platform to urinate into the gutter. I could smell cigarette smoke in the air. I sat quietly listening to them.

'What do you think about those marchers, James?' asked the one who was urinating. His urine was swooshing down the gutter as if the roof was leaking and it was raining hard.

'Wow! That was fun, man, what with the way they were dressed. But most of all I liked the dancing,' came a gruff voice from the cubicle.

'Everything in this country is about the dance nowadays: you want promotion at work, you just dance in the street. You want the reduction of electricity or telephone bills, you go to the street and dance. You want a house, you just dance. You think your boss is a racist, you just dance,' concluded the voice.

'Ha, ha. Then we must also start learning to dance or the gravy train will pass us by.'

'What do they call that dance again?'

'It's called toyi-toyi. You just hop like Bob Marley does on his *Jammin'* song. And that's it. You've made your statement.'

'You bet.'

They laughed and then there was a pause as the guy who had been at the urinal walked over to the tap.

'You know last night I went to confront my cook over the ironing,' he continued. 'I mean she has usually finished the ironing by the time I get home, but yesterday my shirt was still not ironed by nine in the evening.'

'So what did you tell her? That you were going to fire her?'

'No. Because when I burst into her room I found her with some guy, and you know what she told me?'

'Tell me.'

'She said to me politely, "Darling, not only white people enjoy sex". Meaning that I should knock when I enter my room that she is temporarily living in while she is working for me.'

'Tell me you're joking!'

'Seriously.'

I covered my mouth with my hand so that the two guys couldn't hear me laughing.

'Uhh, you don't know how I felt. I was furious.'

'So what happened to the shirt then? Did you iron it yourself?'

'No, I left it there, and in the morning it was nicely ironed and laid out on the sofa.'

'Really? You're joking. So what did you tell her in the morning?'

'Haaa! Can you say anything nowadays? They will just dance that toyi-toyi dance of theirs and call you a racist.'

'You're right. And their government will side with them.'

'Yep. You know sometimes it makes me long for those days. Us white people no longer have a hope in this country,' sighed the guy who was standing by the tap. I heard the water running, followed by the sound of him washing his hands. 'They've got the power now and there's nothing we can do.'

'I even think of moving to Cape Town sometimes. At least down there, things are still fine.'

'All you can do is pretend to befriend them.'

'I think I should go ask Terrence to teach me how to do that toyi-toyi dance so that I can start practising with my kids at home just in case.'

'It won't work, unless you apply some black shoe polish to your face and shave your head. If you can do that and rename yourself Shaka Zulu, then you can demand affirmative action.'

'Imagine that!'

'Yeah. This affirmative action is killing us white people, it's just racism in reverse.'

'You bet.'

I had finished my business inside the cubicle, but I remained seated, afraid that they would notice my presence. I heard their footsteps fading as they went out.

I flushed the toilet and went to wash my hands. There were two cigarette butts in the sink when I ran the water. As I was drying my hands, I suddenly recalled that the Terrence they were referring to was in fact Dunga; that was his Christian name.

twenty-two

At half past three that afternoon Dunga and I walked down the congested street to Park Station to catch the train home. Since I had been chucked out of the Y, I had been travelling every day from Orlando West to campus. Dunga caught the Lenasia train and I caught the Naledi one as we lived in different sections of Soweto, but both of our trains pulled in at the same platform.

My train to Soweto was the first one to pull in. I left Dunga and pushed my way into the third-class carriage, which was already full of commuters. Inside, people were already crammed like sardines, every one of them jostling to find a place to perch in those uncomfortable, suffocating carriages. Some people were even sitting precariously where the two carriages joined.

The hawkers plied their trade from one carriage to another, jostling their way past the other commuters in search of potential customers. At any one time three to four hawkers would be vying for business with each other in the same carriage, carrying the almost identical merchandise.

I managed to find a place to stand with the other straphangers inside as the train slowly pulled out towards Soweto. It was almost impossible to find a space to sit and even if I could have, I don't think that I would have sat down – my guilty conscience would have forced me to let one of the weary senior citizens next to me have the seat.

My nostrils were stung by the odour of sweaty armpits and fading cheap perfumes, dirty shoes and tired mouths. That unwholesome smell filled the length of the crammed yellow and grey Metrorail carriage. But who could blame those wage labourers who had been reduced to walking corpses by their backbreaking labour?

I had deliberately chosen the carriage that was second from the end of the train because as usual there was a religious service going on there. I had this idea that travelling in this carriage I would be able to avoid the pickpockets that run rampant on the trains.

I was also troubled by memories of the train violence that hit Gauteng a few years ago. I had found it difficult to erase the terrible picture I had seen on TV of my neighbour, who had been hacked to death with a panga.

At the time the ruling National Party tried to explain the bloodbath as black-on-black political violence. However, they were not alone in the finger-pointing: the ANC blamed it on the Inkatha Freedom Party and a covert 'third force'. The IFP in turn blamed it on the ANC. Still, it made no difference who was to blame, those who were affected were the ordinary people; thousands were laid to rest almost every day.

Since then I had developed a phobia about using the train. Every time I boarded a train I was seized by the fear of death, and I always prayed to God to help me arrive home safe.

The moment the train left the platform, a middle-aged woman wet her thick dry lips and began to sing a hymn with her Bible clutched against her bust. As the other members of the congregation joined her, the carriage was filled with the soprano voices of almost all of the women inside. It was a familiar Setswana hymn:

Tumelo ke thebe	(Faith is the shield)
Tu-me-lo-ke the-be	
Tsamayang le Jesu	(Go with Jesus)
Tsa-mayang le Jesu	

The singing lasted for about three or four minutes, then the preacher, who was also carrying a Bible, cried 'Hallelujah!' to signal the start of his sermon. He was very dark in complexion, but his hair was almost all white; his face was covered by a beard and moustache that sprouted as if he was a billy-goat. We all responded with an 'Amen' to show that we were ready to drink in his every word. He coughed to prepare his throat before delivering the word of God.

As the preacher began to speak his big adam's apple, which protruded like a golf ball above his half-buttoned blue shirt, bobbed up and down alarmingly. An energetic-looking woman was busy interpreting every sentence, as he was delivering his sermon in Southern Sotho. The commuters-turned-congregation uttered an 'Amen' after each sentence. At regular intervals the preacher would pound his fist down onto his Bible to emphasize a point.

'Oyi Oyi Jesus,' he shouted and rolled his eyes around in his head. 'You know what, bazalwane?' he asked.

'Amen,' the congregation responded.

'I never get tired of reading this book,' he said, laying his hand on the Bible tenderly.

'Amen.'

'You can read your novel, but the only beautiful words are in this holy book.'

'Amen.'

He looked at the two men standing next to me. With some difficulty, one of the two men was busy reading the sport section on the back page of his copy of the *Sowetan*.

'You can read your newspaper, but the only truth is found in this book!'

'Amen!'

'You can read your *True Love* magazine, but the only undying love is in this book!'

'Amen!'

'Praise the Lord!' a woman shouted above everyone in the carriage.

The other members of the congregation turned to look at the woman with amusement written all over their faces.

The preacher wiped the sweat from his forehead. As the train pulled out of Mayfair Station towards Langlaagte a hawker entered our carriage; he had a bloated face and was carrying a white bucket full of beer under an avalanche of ice. He looked very drunk; a crumpled cigarette was stuck behind his ear. An awkward silence fell.

The hawker ignored the preacher and his sermon and cried out his bread-and-butter sales pitch: 'Ezibandayo ngapha! Three rand kuphela! Cold ones here! Only three rand! Cold ones here, nearly for nothing!'

The two men next to me looked at each other and then at the preacher. They began whispering, and then the one who had been reading the sport section tucked his copy of the *Sowetan* under his arm, nudged the hawker and bought two cold long tom Castle cans. I was also tempted to buy a beer to cool off. Stuck inside that overcrowded carriage, cold sweat had begun to drip down my armpits and cramp was beginning to seize my left foot; the carriage was so full that it was difficult for me to even change position. I sucked in the stinking hot air and wet my lips, thinking of that cold beer.

But I instantly forgot the idea when the preacher spied the two men on our side of the carriage and raised his eyebrows questioningly. To make matters worse, as one of the men opened his can of beer the foam splashed onto the preacher's Bible, which he had just opened to read a verse. A blob of foam also landed on the preacher's navy suit.

The preacher gazed at the man with utter disgust. He stopped talking for about forty seconds. Then he took out his handkerchief and wiped the foam off his Bible. The culprit simply whispered, "Sorry baba mfundisi," and continued talking to his friend.

Another chorus started in Sesotho.

Lerato la Jesu	(The love of Jesus)
Le ya-maa-katsa	(It's amaa-zing)
Le yamakatsa	(It's amazing)
Le ya-makatsa	(It's amazing)

Jesu o a re rata	(Jesus loves us)
Ka pelo le moya	(Heart and soul)
Jesu wa ma-katsa	(Jesus is amazing)

The preacher hid his anger and put his handkerchief back inside his pocket. The drunken beer hawker mistook the gesture as that of a potential customer groping in his pocket for money and turned to stare directly at the preacher, while continuing to cry out his sales pitch at the top of his voice. For a moment I also thought that the preacher wanted a beer, but he simply ignored the hawker.

The chorus continued. The hawker peered at the preacher with his bloodshot eyes one last time and turned to leave. I watched him as he jostled through the singing crowd and opened the door to the next carriage, staggering under the weight of his merchandise.

As soon as the singing had stopped the preacher continued with his sermon.

'The devil gave the wicked man alcohol so that he can help him to destroy the Temple of God.' He paused to take a last look at the beer hawker, who by then was in the next carriage. 'Your body is the Temple of God, ladies and gentlemen, which can only be washed clean by the blood of Jesus and not that of Satan. Hallelujah!' He turned to look directly at the two straphangers who had bought the beers.

Silence fell. Our eyes followed those of the preacher's. Beads of sweat began to gather on his temples.

'The devil gave man cigarettes, drugs and guns so that he can help him to renounce The Father and Our Saviour by destroying his Temple. Hallelujah, bazalwane!' He paused again to listen to the response from his congregation.

Just then I inhaled the acrid smell of cigarette smoke, and spotted that one of the two men who had bought beer from the hawker was now busy smoking.

'Eei-eeei-eeeishie!' the preacher sneezed.

'Amen,' responded the congregation.

'No! Bless you, baba mfundisi,' corrected the smoking man behind me.

'Hallelujah!' screamed the preacher. 'The devil gave man condoms so that he can become a prostitute. Hallelujah!'

Soon the congregation began to rhythmically stamp their feet and drum on the walls of the carriage, accompanied by the continuous ringing of a bell. This was a ploy to attract more members to the congregation.

Although I couldn't see out of the crammed carriage, my sense of smell confirmed that we were approaching Croesus Station. There was a powerful smell of yeast from the factory nearby.

The train pulled in at the station and more people rushed into our already crammed carriage. Another hawker entered, carrying cheap perfume in an open brown cardboard box.

The train pulled out of the station towards Longdale Station. Before the hawker could make his sales pitch, a female straphanger who was singing in front of us suddenly stopped and beckoned to him. She asked the price and then reached for her purse to buy some perfume. The preacher hemmed for silence.

'Siyanamukela abasanda kungena. Welcome to those who just entered.' He paused. 'Whoeie, I love this book,' he said, kissing his Bible. 'I just love this book,' he repeated. 'You know why?' He looked around for an answer. 'Isn't it the good book?'

'Blessed be the name of God!' a woman shouted next to me.

'Hallelujah, bazalwane,' the preacher continued. 'A condom is an immoral and misguided weapon to fight HIV and AIDS. Amen, bazalwane.'

'Amen.'

'I'm telling you that we will never have a cure for this disease, ladies and gentleman. Amen, bazalwane.'

'Amen.'

'Those who read God's book, Genesis verse 18-19, will know about the ancient cities of Palestine called Sodom and Gomorrah, which were destroyed for their wickedness. AIDS is a punishment from God because the world today has become wicked. Amen, bazalwane.'

'Glory hallelujah!'

'The reason why a condom bursts when you are having sex outside your marriage shows that sex should only be performed inside the institution of marriage. We need not question God's wisdom. Hallelujah!'

'Amen.'

'If you cheat on your wife or husband, a condom will burst and you will contract AIDS. Hallelujah!'

Laughter followed.

'Amen,' muttered the amused crowd.

'A condom contributes to the breaking down of the institution of marriage and the mutual respect of ubuntu. So, you must start preparing now before you die or before the Creator destroys this wicked world on the day of resurrection. Hallelujah!'

'Amen.'

The train was gliding slowly towards New Canada Station. The preacher paused and looked at his over-attentive congregation with glee. Most of us were smiling at his sermon, which was spiced with humour.

As I was standing there smiling I became interested in the whispered conversation of the two straphangers who were busy drinking and smoking behind me.

'Gaaa, If God can have sons then we are all his sons even if we drink, smoke and commit adultery,' said the one with the newspaper under his arm.

'You know this religion thing surprises me. Ever since I was born every preacher had been preaching the same old thing that Jesus is coming soon. When is soon? I am now forty-seven years old and still they say Jesus is coming. Do you think he is really coming?'

'Never! A dead man is a dead man. Let's just enjoy life while we're still alive. There is no life after death.'

The perfume hawker used this opportunity, while the preacher was ruminating, to make his sales pitch with no holds barred. 'Two rand kuphela kimi. Ten rand e Pick n' Pay. Only two rand from me. Ten rand at Pick n' Pay.'

On the bridge before New Canada Station, we came to a halt to allow the train in front of us enough time at the platform. A woman in front of me who had been counting her loose change plonked a five rand coin down in the hawker's hand in exchange for three bottles of no-name perfume. At that moment the train moved forward towards the platform and the sermon began again.

'God's Kingdom in this earth has been destroyed. Amen, bazalwane. Let us pray for this sick old world. This earth no longer runs by truth and faith, but by the desire for money, by lust and hate. God's Temple in you has been destroyed. Amen, bazalwane.'

Just before the train came to a halt at New Canada Station, the empty long tom Castle cans were fed to the wind through the open window.

'Praise the Lord. Glory hallelujah!' shouted the preacher while closing his Bible and starting a new hymn in Zulu.

As the hymn reached its climax, the woman who had just bought the perfume flung her arms out and looked upwards. She opened her mouth and screamed 'Glory hallelujah', as if God was some deaf idiot sitting somewhere on the roof of the train.

As the train pulled in at the New Canada Station, she fainted and fell on top of the two straphangers next to me, tears streaming down her cheeks. The preacher stopped his sermon and, as the train came to a halt, he and other members of the congregation helped her out of the train and laid her carefully on the cement floor of the platform. With his handkerchief, the preacher tried to fan some fresh air onto the woman's face.

More commuters pushed onto the train as others forced their way onto the platform to board trains to Vereeniging. The big-bodied shouldered and elbowed the weaker ones out of the doorways; to be the first ones to board the train, which stopped for less than a minute and a half at each station. Others ran across the line instead of using the bridge.

As the train pulled out of the New Canada Station, I managed to peer through the window at the horizon, hoping for a whiff of fresh winter air. But all I could see was the murky sky of Soweto, God's worst ghetto, obscured by a layer of smoke from the Welcome Dover coal stoves used by the residents to cook and warm their houses. The smoke from the Welcome Dovers was complemented by that made by the homemade mbawula coal stoves in the tin shacks squashed into the yards of each and every block of Soweto houses.

I remained standing inside the train as it pulled out of the platform toward Mzimhlophe station; the first station inside Soweto on the Naledi line. The commuters were still shoving each other in a final attempt to locate an empty seat, but my mind was still on the noxious smoke that hid the thousands of uniform four-roomed matchbox houses and the shacks between them.

The drab sight of my neighborhood reminded me of a classmate, who had been in my political studies tutorial group, and who had passed away the previous weekend. He and six members of his family were killed in their sleep by the inhalation of coal smoke from their mbawula stove in their Orange Farm shack.

Yerr, I admitted to myself when I saw the smoke, *living in constant contact with danger has become normal for the five million people who live in God's worst ghetto.*

My thoughts were interrupted by another hymn that had started in Zulu. It had a nice rhythm.

Avulekile amasango	(The gates are open)
Ayaya. Ayaya	
Asezulwini	(Of heaven)
Ayaya. Ayaya	
Sigeza izono	(We wash the sins)
Ngegazi	(With blood)

179

Thina sibuye mnqamlezweni	(We from the end of the country)
Sikhululekilee	(We are free)
Sigeza izono	(We wash the sins)
Ngegazi	(With blood)
Hoza sisi nawe	(Come you also sister)
Hoza buti nawe	(Come you also brother)

The singing inside the carriage continued as the train moved towards Mzimhlophe station. Another preacher, this time a woman, had taken over and was delivering her sermon in English; the male preacher had remained on New Canada Station.

'Praise the Lord. Glory hallelujah!' she shouted.

'Amen.'

'The love of Jesus to you is very great. Sometimes preachers can leave me baffled; like this past Saturday at the Avalon cemetery. It was at the funeral of a thug who had been killed by the police in a shootout after a hijack. The preacher who was handling the funeral told the attendants that God giveth and now taketh his son again. How could the loving Father kill his own son? God does not kill, but he loves. Amen, bazalwane.' She paused and bit her lower lip in thought.

The train stopped at the Mzimhlophe Station. Hundreds of commuters disembarked including half of the people that filled our carriage. The female preacher tapped her head with her forefinger to allow the noise to subside. As the train pulled away the congregation began to sing again, but she then hemmed for them to stop. She wiped some sweat that had begun to form on her forehead.

'Yes, bazalwane. That thug was killed because of the life he had chosen for himself. He had renounced God as his Father and followed the devil's ways of lust, envy and lies. How do you still call such a person the son of God? The son of God does not do such bad things. Hallelujah, bazalwane.'

The preacher paused again and looked around, there were nods of consent from most of the commuters.

'Some people still take the evangel for granted. Those people think that on the day of resurrection people will simply be asked to choose between two paths – one to heaven and one to hell – as simple as that. I overheard one man on the day of the funeral telling his friend that going to heaven is just a matter of luck. This is not a joke, bazalwane,' she said, as some of her congregation started to laugh. 'There are still people amongst us who think that going to heaven is like the lottery. The man at the funeral said to his friend that he would simply avoid whichever path Adolf Hitler, Verwoerd, Idi Amin and Stalin take on the day of the resurrection.' She paused and smiled as some members of the congregation began to laugh. 'If it was that simple why should we continue preaching? We might as well throw our Bibles into the river. You will hear the sinners say that heaven must be boring, a monotonous life of singing and an unchanging menu of milk and honey. Some of them say that since they are allergic to milk and honey they would rather choose the devil because they like eating meat. They would say that they would rather eat other human flesh together with Satan than go to heaven. I'm telling you now that the choice is here on earth. There won't be time to repent on that fateful day.'

The crowd beamed with amusement. Some began to stand up so that they could leave the train at Phefeni station. I was already standing next to the door, as it was my stop. The preacher continued: 'Some people think they can bribe the officials at the gates of hell for an immediate transfer to heaven if they can't stand the heat down there. If you believe that you are a fool. Even if you are rich like Bill Gates or Michael Jackson you cannot use the money to bribe the angels to let you into heaven. Money and bribes are just earthly things that will be destroyed on doomsday. Who wants to sit on the right hand of Jesus?' she asked. And without pausing for an answer she asked another question: 'Who wants to suffer for eternity frying in the fires of hell? Ladies and gentlemen, you must start preparing now. Remember, there are only six more years left before the millennium.'

Darkness had already enveloped the awkward V-shaped asbestos roofs of my neighbourhood as I left the train. I could see a glimmer coming from the small windows in each indistinguishable four-roomed house. I lit up my cigarette. My unzipped parka billowed around me in the chilly wind. Inhaling the stress-relieving smoke I started to wonder if God was indeed multilingual. Just face the truth: every second The Man Upstairs hears almost every language in the world from his children.

How does Zulu sound to God? I asked myself. *Is it aggressive or romantic? I can hear every preacher saying that there is only one God we must direct our prayers to. But does he have good interpreters like the woman in the train interpreted the preacher's Sesotho? Does The Man understand tsotsitaal, or are we just wasting our time praying to Him in that language?*

I was convinced that God was white, and either English or Afrikaans, simply because it had taken Him so many years to get an interpreter to translate exactly what the blacks and the poor wanted in their endless prayers. It took God almost a century to bring about the end of apartheid and its package of injustice and to usher in the long-awaited freedom. It also seemed to me that English and Afrikaans are God's languages. Mastering those two languages in our country had since become the only way to avoid the poverty of twilight zones like Soweto.

The grubby horizon had given birth to a dark winter evening. I walked with about eighty commuters in single file towards the gates. The Metro ticket inspectors were standing there to verify that we had genuine tickets. Next to them were about a dozen police officers, waiting for the slightest opportunity to arrest defaulters. As I walked through the tunnel under the line with the other commuters I saw another hawker carrying a small cardboard box filled with chalk for killing cockroaches making his last sales pitch of the day. I passed the Sisulu Clinic by the main road and ignored the flash of light that streaked out from an oncoming car as I jaywalked towards my home.

twenty-three

We were on the main road through Orlando West, next to the Hector Peterson commemorative stone and opposite Uncle Tom's Hall. Dunga's forefinger pointed down to stop taxis bound for Bara Hospital.

That's how it's done in the township. Fingers are the only means of communication between the driver of a minibus-taxi and the commuter on the street. If you're in Soweto and your fore-finger points skywards it means you're going to town (Johannesburg). If you lift both your middle and forefinger it means you're going to Highgate Mall. Five fingers means that you are probably lost because it means Lenasia, which is in the opposite direction.

The midday taxi was empty and we both sat up front with the driver as he hooted at all the pedestrians on the side of the road, trying to find passengers to fill up his taxi. Through the windscreen I could see the July wind raising red dust across the valley on the untarred side streets of Orlando East.

As we crossed over the railway bridge that links the East and West sections of Orlando we passed a large red and white bill-board on the side of the road:

PEPSI WELCOMES YOU TO ORLANDO EAST

Along Mooki Street, which is the first street in Orlando East after the railway bridge, the taxi turned left in the direction of Orlando Station.

'Short left!' shouted Dunga to the driver before the police station. That's the way to stop a taxi in Soweto; 'short left' simply means that you're getting out of the taxi at the next street on the left.

Slowly Dunga and myself walked past the police station and crossed Mooki Street before we got to the post office. Ahead of us a crowd was standing in a circle.

'I wonder what's happening there?' said Dunga.

'I wonder too. Look! Can you see police over there?' I said, pointing at the three police vans next to the crowd.

We jostled our way through the crowd to assess the situation for ourselves. In the centre there were three people lying motionless with deep gashes all over their bodies. Their clothes were soaked with blood and one of the victims was still choking out a death rattle. Next to the victims were all sorts of weapons that had been used by the angry crowd of men, women and children. I saw pangas, spades, pick handles, axes and garden forks. For some reason I was immediately reminded of a biblical film I had watched when I was about five years old, in which Stephen was stoned to death for spreading the word of God.

'By the way, this is the township,' Dunga said, as if to remind himself. 'Life is cheap and death is absolutely free of charge.'

'But it's a cruel thing to end another man's life in this painful way,' I said, as if I knew of a better way of dying.

'What have they done?' Dunga asked one of the vigilantes.

'They are thieves,' she answered with one brief uninterested look at Dunga.

'But where were the police?'

'Don't tell me about those bastards – all they know about is taking bribes and buying stolen goods themselves,' said the vigilante angrily.

About ten police officers were busily taking an official statement from one of the senior citizens standing there. But it was obvious that by the time they arrived the three victims were already somewhere between heaven and hell, although the police station was just down the road.

As we stood there, I caught a glimpse of one of the victims' bloodstained face. My heart sank as I realised that his damaged face was familiar to me. He was one of the guys who had come to my home on the day of the national elections to negotiate the sale of some sound equipment. I looked at Dunga to see whether he had also recognised the man.

'So crime indeed pays,' Dunga whispered.

'Yeah, they were caught at their game.'

'Remember what I was telling Themba the day he bought those stolen goods?'

In a wink we were out of the mob, for fear that the victims might miraculously come back to life and point us out as their customers.

As soon as we were out of the crowd Dunga and myself were faced with the task of finding the house to which the undertaker Mr Skhosana had given Dunga directions. He had called Dunga the night before and confirmed that he had a Njomane on his list. But in all my years living inside this abject pit of red earth called Soweto I have learnt that asking residents for directions by citing a street name is like flogging a dead horse. People down here have a strange way of understanding their environment. They associate their neighbourhood with something distinctive: a school, church, or shebeen will be used as a landmark rather than a street name. If you insist on a street name, I swear that the residents of this place might unwittingly misdirect you, even if you are just a few metres away from your destination.

One of the reasons that street names are out of fashion in Soweto is that most of the streets are dusty and muddy, and therefore nothing to be proud of. The majority of them are without road signs; their names are written on the walls of the houses at the corners. If you happen to be the owner of a house on which a street name appears and want to give your house a new look by plastering it, you would be unwittingly wiping the street name off the map. But you cannot plaster over the memory that a shebeen operates there.

Dunga took the piece of paper from his pocket and studied the directions again. The house was number 69298 Sithole Street.

As we walked past the Orlando East YWCA towards the shops, I stepped in a heap of fresh dog shit, and swore under my breath at my misfortune.

I tried to scrape off the shit, which was already caked on my Hi-Tec running shoe, on a projecting stone. I managed to remove a bit of it, but the smell was awful. Dunga was facing the shops, trying to get to downward of the smell.

'Let's buy some smokes first,' he said as we walked towards the shops.

'Damn right!' I said, disgusted.

Next to the fish and chip shop I noticed a heap of rubbish: used plastic bags, old shoes, rags, broken bottles, banana and orange peels. Five stray dogs were fighting over a bone. Further up the street some kids were playing with a plastic ball on a heap of ashy spoil.

As I stared in fascination at the kids, I was nearly run down by an ambling horse hitched to a coal cart. The driver was black with coal dust – even if I had known him well I wouldn't have recognised him. Trying to avoid a car that was coming hell for leather down the street with the music system blaring, the driver turned his horse towards us. Luckily Dunga grabbed me by the hand and I managed to avoid the cart, but slipped on the slime coming from a leaking pipe. The driver of the car didn't even stop or turn his head to examine the confusion that he had caused.

'You poes!' I cursed.

'Hey! Be careful!' warned Dunga. 'This is the township. These soulless sons of bitches have too much money and think they can drive cars without using the brakes.'

'Yeh. You're right,' I replied, trying to joke with him, but the panic had already mushroomed inside me.

Two overloaded minibuses coming from opposite directions started hooting at the driver of the coal cart to give way, but the driver simply ignored them.

'Amalahle, fifteen rand a bag,' he howled at top of his voice, facing the shacks at the side of the road.

He cruelly cracked his whip on the back of the poor horse; the five thin dogs that I'd seen fighting each other on the rubbish heap started chasing and barking at the cart.

Outside the fish and chip shop was a so-called mini-market with hawkers displaying merchandise. A woman with massive, pendulous breasts stood behind a long piece of rusty corrugated tin that had been flattened and was supported by two large stones at each end. A small umbrella was unfurled above her; I didn't understand why because the sun wasn't hot at all. As we drew nearer I noticed that her armpits were drenched with perspiration. *Maybe it's from cutting the meat?* I reasoned. Some haphazardly cut meat was arranged in rows in front of her on the corrugated tin. Only the saleslady knew whether it was horse, sheep, cattle or dog meat.

At the edge of the woman's stall was the head of a black cow, its horns still attached, dripping with blood. The cow's tongue, which hung from its mouth, was crawling with flies; at regular intervals the saleslady tried desperately to stop the flies from enjoying the carcass by using the back of her hand to chase them away. Dunga looked at that dead cow's head and began laughing.

'What are you laughing at?' I asked.

'My mother once told me an old story of a man and a cow. Do you know it?'

'No. Tell me.'

'It goes like this. One day in the rural area of KwaZulu where she comes from, a man was so sick and tired of life that he decided it was better to end his own life. He took his rope to the bushes where the cattle graze. After finding a nice tree to hang himself, he tied his rope around a branch and put the noose around his neck. After a few minutes of dangling from the tree and choking to death, a cow came from the nearby bush and loosened the rope from the branch with its horns. The man fell down; he was still alive although he had already shat himself. The cow waited until the man regained consciousness, and then it began to plead with him. It said: "Man, please don't do anything stupid like killing yourself. You know that according to your culture when you die one of us has to be killed to feed the hungry mourners. You see, I'm starting to gain weight and enjoying my life. If you die I'll probably be the target". And from that day that man swore to himself never to entertain thoughts of killing himself again.'

I laughed as hard as I could. 'I never thought that cows in Kwa-Zulu could speak!'

While we were standing there talking, a kid came by to buy a few kilos of meat. As the woman leaned forward to grab the rusty jagged-edged knife that was lying next to a large chunk of meat and an axe, her left breast spilled out of her half-buttoned shirt. She pushed it back inside her grubby white shirt, which was spotted with blood, and began to cut some meat.

As she sawed at the carcass her breast swayed from side to side and once again began to spill out of her shirt. Annoyed, she tried to push it back. I watched her surreptitiously as she continued cutting the carcass, and once again her breast swayed from side to side, but this time she didn't bother to stop it falling out of her shirt and the tip of her nipple touched the meat.

Having succeeded, she used her scales to weigh the meat, then wrapped it in an old newspaper. She exchanged the meat for the twenty rand note that the kid was holding in his hand.

Next to the butchery was a small traditional surgery. A traditional healer was standing in front of his mat, which was covered in every sort of traditional medicine. There were roots, leaves, ochre and herbs in small bottles as well as shells from the ocean. As soon as we passed him, the medicine man sprang up.

'This,' he shouted, holding up a small bottle with black liquid inside, 'boys, is a love potion; it can charm every lady you want in the world. If you want Miss Soweto, you must drink this. If you want Miss South Africa, you must have this bottle. If you want Miss Universe, buy this from me.'

I laughed hard and nudged Dunga, who laughed as well. The

medicine man put the small bottle down, smiled at us and pointed at some sun-dried leaves.

'Ai-eei-aitshie! This will help you pass your exam,' sniffed the medicine man, as if he knew that I was in the area for that reason. He wiped his nose with the back of his hand. 'Which one do you want, boys? I've got everything; muti for impotency, low libido, weak erections, early ejaculations, AIDS-prevention medicine, headaches, stomach-aches, cancer, malaria, pregnancy; every-thing, boys!'

'Not today, baba,' said Dunga.

Next to him a girl of about fifteen sat behind a large bowl of raw fish. Beside her bowl were two cigarette packets and five boxes of matches. She was busy breastfeeding her crying baby, and looked as if she was about to cry herself. There were flies all over the face of the baby; they were enjoying their breakfast of sleep from the baby's eyes and snot from its nose. When she'd chase them away they would immediately settle in the bowl of raw fish. They seemed to be playing games with her, always choosing to be where she didn't want them to be. At one stage I saw two large green flies mating on the lower lip of her crying baby while the girl was still busy chasing the others off the raw fish.

As Dunga and I waited to buy loose cigarettes, a man wearing a grimy blue overall came over from the other side of the road. He bent forward and took two cigarettes from one of the opened packets. I watched him as he lit one with a match.

'How much do I owe you so far?' asked the man as he inhaled the smoke from his cigarette.

'Four rand fifty,' answered the girl timidly.

'Oh no! You can't rob me,' said the man. 'Do you think I'm a bank?'

'But buti Siphiwe, you took nine cigarette pieces from me this week,' the girl pleaded.

'I'm only joking,' said the man smiling again. 'I'll settle my debt tomorrow.' Puffing his cigarette, he crossed back over the road and went into a scrapyard, where there was a heap of old cars. Four other men in their greasy work coats were busy welding; the sputtering sound that came from the yard was deafening and the workmen all talked at top of their voices. One of the scrap cars was standing on top of two large stones that were being used as jacks. *I wonder where those cars come from?* part of me was asking. *Probably they are hijacked cars that are being tampered with to change their identity.*

At that moment a police van passed along the dusty road, but the police officers inside it didn't look at the scrapyard.

Dunga dug deep into his pockets and came out with a two rand coin. He gave it to the girl with the baby in exchange for four loose cigarettes.

'Where can I find a toilet?' I asked the girl as she took the money from Dunga.

'For A or B?'

'What's that?'

'If you want to sit you have to go inside the shop and ask. But if you want to stand then you can go there,' answered the girl, pointing to the corner of the shop.

'I want to stand.'

'Just go there, at that corner there.'

'I'll join you,' said Dunga.

Dunga lit a cigarette and we both walked down the side of the shop where the girl had pointed. Behind the shop a group of about eight men squatted in a circle on the red soil, busy playing dice. A small heap of money was lying in the centre of that circle.

'Oh pop! Oh pop! Oh four three! Oh five two!' shouted the man who was throwing the two dice in the centre of that little crowd.

We ignored the men and walked over to the wall to piss. The ground was still wet with urine from the men playing dice. The smell of shit and urine was almost unbearable, although it was diluted by the noxious smell of burning tires somewhere behind

190

the shacks. Next to where Dunga was standing, the remains of a burnt tire also blackened the soil.

Within a few seconds, a short, big-bellied, middle-aged man joined us. He was wearing several thick gold chains around his neck. A pile of shit that lay on the yellowish grass separated the man and myself.

Another tall guy who was smoking dagga also joined us at the wall. What embarrassed me was that, besides the fact that we were in plain view, the man next to me was busy wolf-whistling some gorgeous ladies who happened to be passing by in the street. The ladies seemed to know him because they came over and stood behind us.

He finished peeing before I did and wagged his big black circumcised penis viciously until the last drop of urine fell on the back of his hand. He put his penis back inside his trousers and zipped them up. As he did this, a dung beetle mounted the man's lace-up C & J designer shoe, rolling its round cake of human shit with its hind legs. The man shook his leg and the beetle fell to ground and lost its prize. As he turned to join the three laughing ladies who were still standing there, he stepped on the ball of human shit that the beetle had made. He didn't even notice.

Dunga and myself made our way towards the thick black smoke, taking one of the long and winding paths in between the shacks. On each washing-line some clothes dangled, dripping with water. As we passed one of the lines two dogs barked at us. The woman who was dandling her baby outside the shack shouted, 'Voetsek, Spotty!' and the dogs slunk away without biting us. We walked on ash and clinker which had been spread on the path between the half-open shacks.

After a few minutes we crossed a slimed road. On the wall of the corner house was a sign: Sithole Street. There was a number on the back door as well and Dunga started counting: '69293, 69294, 69295'. He counted until we came to number 69298. It was a three-roomed house with six shacks occupying every inch

191

of the yard. I was sure as hell that I wouldn't remember how to get there if I had to come back alone some day.

A surprised grey-haired old woman, who introduced herself as Ma Mhlongo, answered our knock at the door; although she welcomed us warmly I couldn't help but notice two fat cockroaches milling leisurely around a hunk of brown bread that was abandoned on top of an old plank. Four others were hiding in the cracks of one of the homemade kitchen units. *Ag shit!* I exclaimed disgustedly to myself when a kid came by, took the piece of bread, and disappeared again.

Dunga and myself seated ourselves on the bench in the kitchen. I could see six or seven loose projecting nails; we had to be careful where we sat because those nails could easily tear our trousers.

'Afternoon, Mama; my name is Dunga and this is Dingz,' said Dunga, showing the woman his work card. His name and picture appeared on that card. The woman just looked at the picture and gave us a confused smile. 'We both work for the new ANC government,' he said, taking a forged form out from a file.

The woman beamed at the mention of the ANC, as if we were there to deliver their promises. She didn't even bother looking at the card that Dunga showed her and he quickly put it back into his pocket.

'Sanibona, bantwabami. Hello, my children,' she said, still beaming with happiness.

'Mama. What we are doing is this, we are busy registering the names of the orphans in this township so that they can receive monthly grants from the government to help you feed them.'

'That is a very good thing that the government is doing for us. Only three months in office and already you are prepared to help the poor. I will always vote for you,' said the woman with all her heart.

'We checked with undertaker Skhosana there by the Masakhane Funeral Parlour and he informed us that Ntokozo Njomane, who passed away in April, was your daughter, and that she left three kids who are fatherless.'

'Oh! Mntanami. My son,' began the woman with grief in her eyes. 'That is true. It is very difficult to feed and clothe the children with my pension. I don't know how to thank you if you can get me the grant you are talking about. Thanks to that kind gentleman baba Skhosana as well.'

'All we need is a copy of her death certificate for the records, Mama. But remember that this might take some time to come about,' said Dunga.

'I know my son. I'm willing to wait,' said the woman as she stood up. She called someone in the dining-room. 'Nomfundo! Please bring me the yellow plastic bag under my bed.'

'I will, Ma. Just let me dry my hair,' answered a female voice.

From the dining-room I could hear splashing water: the lady was busy taking a bath.

Suddenly a barefoot kid, who was wearing worn-out shorts that exposed his pale bum, passed us and tried to open the dining-room door. As soon as he turned the handle I heard a torrent of abuse from the lady inside. For a few seconds the insults brought silence in the kitchen; the old woman wearily shook her grey-haired head.

'These children! I don't know why they don't go and play outside like other children do. That is the deceased's second-born,' said the old woman, pointing at the stunned kid. She looked at the kid and shouted, 'Leave that door alone and go outside to play!'

As he left she began to confide in us. 'He is a naughty kid and I wonder if he will ever make it to school.'

'Don't worry. He'll change as soon as he grows up,' I tried to console her.

'Well. I hope so,' she said, sounding unconvinced.

Two more kids entered. 'These two are the children of my second-born, the one who comes after the deceased,' said the woman uninterestedly.

'Is that the one in the dining-room?' enquired Dunga.

'No, my son. Nobody knows where she is. She left the house

four days ago and we haven't seen her since,' answered the woman disgustedly. 'The one that is taking the bath inside has at least got some brains,' she said proudly. 'Immediately after divorcing her abusive third husband she went out hunting for a job. She is now working at the kitchens in Randburg. Although she's paid next to nothing she can at least support her four children.'

'That's better,' said Dunga.

'You're right. With these other two it is very difficult,' said the woman in a pitiful voice, shaking her head again. 'I don't know what they'll do if the Lord decides to terminate my contract in this world because they all depend on my pension. The other one is pregnant again and I wonder if she even knows who the father is.'

By and by I could smell expensive perfume from the dining-room, and a lady opened the door. I glanced up at her and our eyes met. She was wearing a tight pair of designer blue jeans, a crimson designer T-shirt and some black leather stilettos. She came out carrying a large plastic bowl half full of dirty water. She muttered 'hi' and, without waiting for our response, walked outside. I heard the water splashing heavily against the soil and then she was back, empty-handed.

'Nomfundo, where is that plastic bag I asked you to bring from the room? These people have been waiting and we must not delay them. Orlando East is very big.'

'OK, Ma; I'm sorry,' apologised Nomfundo as she quickly went back into the dining-room.

In two ticks she was back with a yellow plastic bag. The old woman undid the knot tied in it and took out some papers. Nomfundo helped her as she searched through them, but it didn't take long before the old woman found a paper and handed it to Dunga. I felt relieved, having finally secured the death certificate I needed – but to our surprise it was just an obituary from a programme printed by the Masakhane Funeral Parlour.

'Mama, I mean the paper that you got from the Home Affairs

194

office, not from Mr Skhosana,' said Dunga. 'That paper is so important that there is nothing that out government can do without it.'

There was no death certificate in that plastic bag. Nomfundo gave us a pleading smile and went into the dining-room with her mother to do some more searching.

About forty-five minutes elapsed while we waited for them to find the death certificate, but to no avail. The old woman came back with sadness in her eyes.

'Please my children, come back next week, I think by then I will have found it.'

twenty-four

My grip was surely slipping. I thought I had already lost my hold. Although I was watching an old Bruce Lee movie, *Enter the Dragon*, on SABC 1, my mind was busy trying to come up with a plan to secure an aegrotat. In front of me on the table was a Hansa Pilsner quart that I had just bought from Theks's home; there were three more cold ones in the fridge.

I was still trying to figure it all out when the phone rang. I looked at my wristwatch; the hands were creeping towards midnight. *Could it be that the family found the death certificate and decided to ring me at this time of the night?* I asked myself. *Maybe Dunga has had another idea of how to help me.* I picked up the phone.

'Wola kawu, it's me.' It was Dworkin's drunken voice, accompanied by a lot of background noise.

'Are you OK, my son?' His safety leapt into my mind.

'Very OK, my son. Tell me, did you manage to get that stupid death certificate?'

'No, I didn't. But I have promises.'

'I'm sorry, son.'

'Where are you this time of the morning?'

'Let me see,' he began uncertainly. 'I'm here in Windhoek at the Southern Comfort Hotel along Castle Street.'

I assumed that Windhoek must be another new nickname for a section of Vosloorus.

'Who's that waking us up when we are sleeping?' It was my aunt, who was peering out from behind her half-open door.

'It's Dunga,' I lied, covering the mouthpiece of the phone with my hand. My aunt shook her large grey head and went back inside her room. 'So why didn't you come as you promised?' I asked, feigning disappointment. 'Dunga and myself have been waiting for you.'

'I'm sorry, son, but I couldn't miss the opportunity of meeting the international visitors in our area. Jack Daniel's and Captain Morgan were the masters of ceremony and I wanted to get their autographs.'

I was lost. 'Oh! I see.'

'Yeah, son. There were also these British singers called Spiced Gold and they rummed our Red Hearts. Themba got VO'd and decided to sink the Black,' he rapped.

'The Spice Girls were there as well?' I asked, astonished by the news. 'Why wasn't it in the media? Where is Themba now?'

'He is sitting with four gorgeous chicks and one of them looks just like Tequila, son. Their names are Dolley's, Savanna, Redd's and Crown.'

'And what's all that noise?'

'It is the international launch of the new branch leader of S.A.D.U. in my area. I wish you were here, son.' He laughed. 'I'm completely, prodigiously, vertically and horizontally drunk, my son.'

It was only then that I realized that Dworkin was calling from a shebeen where he was busy drinking beer with Themba.

The movie and my third bottle of Hansa Pilsner finished almost at the same time. I pushed the sofa aside and rolled out the sponge mattress that I sleep on, but I wasn't ready to sleep. I sat on the sofa and counted the cents in my pocket. Wow! I still had thirteen rand and a few cents.

I opened the fourth and last beer that was in the fridge – it was nice and cold – and began digesting Dunga's advice. His first plan was to be patient and wait for the family to find the death certificate. In the meantime, he suggested that he telephone the dean and pretend to be my uncle. He would tell the dean that he was still waiting for the authority from the other elders of my family to dispose of the deceased's belongings, which were still sacred. We planned to complicate everything with tradition, and if the dean refused we would accuse him of something to do with race discrimination. I wasn't that comfortable with Dunga's first plan. The second plan involved bribery. I was much happier with that. Dunga had given me about two hundred rand and the plan was to bribe the clerk at the Department of Home Affairs on Plein Street to grant me a death certificate. He had told me that as it was some days after their payday, the clerks would probably be broke. According to him, they would accept any money that I could offer them. Since disappointment sometimes drives a man to desperate measures, my mind was already running through the possibilities of Dunga's second plan.

It's About Time by the hot kwaito group Boom Shaka interrupted my thoughts. I watched the TV with great interest as the two ladies from the group shook their ATMs. I looked at the condoms on the table that I'd taken out of my pocket with my change and thought of Nkanyi. The last time I had had sex with her was during the week when no one was at home. It was during the day in my brother's room while he was still at work. We did it and quickly made up his bed so it didn't look like anything had happened. That was our only option since I had forfeited my privacy at the Y.

It was already twenty to one in the morning, but Nkanyi's home was within walking distance. I removed my watch and put on some old clothes so that I didn't attract any criminals on my way to nearby Dube. Very carefully, I closed the door so that my aunt didn't hear me leaving the house; I didn't want her to be angrier with me than she already was. I had already defied her number one rule by putting beers in her fridge on a Sunday, and by drinking them.

The lights on Vilakazi Street were glowing. A few people were standing on the street and I could smell dagga under the tree next to the shops.

'Wola, Dingz,' shouted one of the guys under the tree. I immediately recognized him as Neo, Theks's brother.

'Heita,' I shouted.

'So, where to now?'

'My girlfriend's place.'

198

'For sure. Yizo, mfowethu.'

'Sure, gazi.'

'Give me two rand.'

'Sure.'

I searched my pocket for some coins. I had to give the money to him as a protection fee for my safety on the street. Otherwise they would rob me when I came back. I waited in the middle of the street for Neo to come and take the money. He came over to me smoking a zol. I gave him three rand.

'Sure, ngamla,' he thanked me. 'Skuif?'

'No, you know I don't smoke zol.'

'Just two pulls and you won't feel the distance.'

'Well,' I hesitated. 'Ag, let me have two pulls.'

'Sure, mzala,' said Neo, 'the zol will give you stamina with your girlfriend.'

I took the zol from Neo and took a drag. I coughed three times, choking, and tears rolled down both my cheeks. Neo laughed at me, took the zol and went back to his friends. I felt nothing; I thought it would change something in my mind, but it didn't do anything. I continued walking until I reached Nkanyi's place. All the lights in her house were out except the outside one that faced the street. I knew that her father wasn't there – he was working night duty for Springbok security somewhere in town. I climbed the wall with a bit of difficulty and knocked on the window of the room where she slept with her eleven-year-old sister Amanda. After three knocks her little sister drew the curtains. She smiled. She liked to strike childish contracts with me each time I took her sister back to my place. Amanda opened the window and we began whispering.

'Where is she?'

'Sleeping.'

'Wake her up.'

The little devil looked at me and I knew she wanted something. I searched my pockets and gave her two rand. Without a word

Amanda shook her head. She wasn't moved. I looked again and found another rand. She smiled and put on the light.

'Why come so late?' whispered Nkanyi.

'I couldn't sleep and I was missing you, that's all.'

Her little sister smiled. 'Go with him,' she whispered to her sister, 'I'll be fine.'

Nkanyi rubbed the corners of her eyes. 'What time is it?'

'I don't know,' I answered. 'Past one I guess.'

I watched her dressing. I felt around again and came up with another two rand and gave it to Amanda.

'I want her back here at seven o'clock sharp. Daddy comes home around eight,' she whispered in my ear.

'You got it.'

Silently Nkanyi climbed out of the room into the cold night. She had the key to the gate and we crept quietly out of the garden. There was no sound on the street except the distant barking of dogs, and we walked together arm in arm until we reached my home.

We had to wait outside a bit because the light in the kitchen was on and we were going to sleep in the dining-room. Nkanyi had slept over several times and no one seemed to notice or care. Luckily my two brothers left for work at five and they didn't switch on the lights. Besides, there was the sofa and the table to block their view. Everybody else woke up late and Nkanyi would be gone by then.

I gave Nkanyi my cap to wear. As soon as the light in the kitchen went out I turned the key in the door.

'Dingz, is that you?' my aunt asked from inside her room.

'Yes, it's me.'

'Where have you been? Dworkin called for you.'

'Oh, I was at Theks's place.'

'He said you must call him back tomorrow,' she said. 'I switched the TV off because I thought you had forgotten.'

'Ok, thanks; goodnight.'

twenty-five

That Monday morning the trains were delayed for about an hour. A man had been electrocuted on a pylon between Phefeni and Dube stations. About five electricians were busy working to remove the body. The 132-kilovolt charge had killed him while he was trying to steal copper cable during the night. The electrocuted man was still in his blue overalls, his left foot on the last rung of the steel ladder that was leant against the pylon and his right foot suspended in the air as if he was still engaged in his criminal act. There were lots of people watching as the electricians tried to remove the man's body. From where Nkanyi and myself were standing we could hear the voices of the bystanders.

'Shoo, shoo!' exclaimed one woman with surprise. 'I wonder whose husband is that?'

'How could he risk his life for such a thing?' asked someone else.

'You can sell that thing for a fortune, my bra,' replied another man.

Nkanyi was on her way to campus and I was going to the Home Affairs office in town. She had woken up at my place, but I had taken her back home at about six, before her father came home from his security job. Her mother wasn't as strict with her; she knew that her daughter didn't sleep at home sometimes and didn't mind.

I had dressed in my best formal clothes. I knew that when you need help as quickly as possible, in any office, your dress code is important. First impressions count. And so I was wearing a blue double-breasted jacket that my brother had given me, a white shirt, black tie, black pants and a black pair of highly polished QC shoes. In my right hand I carried a maroon briefcase. I looked as if I was going to some serious business meeting at the JSE.

The train finally arrived at about half past nine; by twenty to ten we were at Park Station. I got out to go to the Home Affairs office while Nkanyi continued her journey to Doornfontein Station.

It was about ten minutes after ten on that cold July morning when I entered the Department of Home Affairs office on Plein Street. There were already about eighty people inside and they were all waiting to be helped by a single clerk behind the counter. Behind the clerk were shelves full of ledgers that were as thick as the casebooks in the Oliver Schreiner Law Library, some of them lying open on the long counter.

'Birth certificates in the first line, marriage and divorce certificates in the second line, death certificates in the last line,' commanded the clerk from behind the counter.

The queue for marriage and divorce certificates was very long. I joined the death certificate queue, where there were about twenty people waiting. I began to feel sorry for the solitary man behind the counter because all the people were waiting for his attention.

Inside my jacket pocket was an obituary of a person I didn't even know. *There are only two ways to end this struggle; a defeat or a victory,* I encouraged myself, *and I am not prepared for defeat*. I took out the obituary and read it for the first time.

Josephine Ntokozo Njomane. *Born 13 June 1962, in Mtubatuba, KwaZulu-Natal. Died on the 17ᵗʰ of April 1994. She is survived by her Mother, three sisters and three children. She will be buried today Saturday the 30ᵗʰ of April 1994 at Avalon Cemetery. Cortege leaves at 9am.*

Forty-five minutes later the queue had swelled and now extended towards the door. There was still only one clerk behind the counter and he was swearing at everybody as if he was the Minister of Home Affairs himself. At eleven o'clock he just left everybody standing there and took a well-deserved break.

While we were all waiting for the clerk to come back from his tea break, which was supposed to be only fifteen minutes, I killed time by talking with the woman in front of me in the queue. She told me that the clerk had been working on his own since she had first come to the office the week before, and that every day he would close the office at around half past three without helping most of the people.

Another woman in the birth certificate queue joined in the conversation. She lambasted the office for lacking respect for black people. She was in that queue to have her date of birth altered on her identity document. According to her pitiful account, she couldn't get a pension because her age was wrongly recorded.

'These are not my years,' said the woman in Zulu, shaking the identity documents that she was holding. 'I was born during the year of the great drought. We were eating yellow mealie-meal at that time. All this office was concerned about when they issued me this document was that I would vote for them. Now that the elections are over and they have won they no longer care about us. We are useless to them. We are like dogs. Huw, huw, huw!' concluded the woman angrily, trying to bark like a dog.

The clerk came back from his tea break at twelve. I wasn't surprised at that – government employees have the luxury of extending their tea breaks whenever they want. The two women I had been talking to were tired of standing and had decided to sit down instead.

At about twenty past twelve a beautiful lady showed up. She didn't bother going to the tail of the queue but went directly to the counter as if she was a member of staff.

'Can I help you?' asked the clerk.

'Yes, sweetheart, can you get me the divorce file from January last year,' she said with a lazy smile.

Without even apologizing to the old man he was busy helping the clerk jumped to the lady's request and put a thick ledger marked 'Divorce 1993' in front of her. I started to boil with anger – I had been there since ten that morning waiting for his assistance. I watched with utter disgust as he told the lady to fill in the form, then bring it back to him to sign and send to the computer people to make a certificate.

After spending another half an hour in the queue, I withdrew and went to the counter for immediate service just like the lady had. If he refused to help me, I thought I would just slip a hundred rand note into one of the ledgers that were lying everywhere on top of the counter, then hand the ledger to the clerk. To my surprise the clerk obviously hadn't seen me waiting in the queue.

'Which file are you looking for, sir?'

His respectful greeting gave me an idea. I suddenly decided to pose as a lawyer. If he asked I would say that my client Miss Njomane died intestate and there was a dispute over who was to benefit from her assets. If he asked me my name I would give him Dunga's business card. I would also tell him that the certificate was due in the High Court in about thirty minutes time. If he still refused, I would threaten him with a subpoena for perverting the course of justice; I would do whatever it took.

'I'm actually looking for a death certificate for my client at the High Court,' I lied.

'It must be a very busy day at the court today,' said the guy while he searched for the ledger on the shelves behind him. 'The lady who was here just now wanted a divorce certificate for her client as well. She is an advocate at the Johannesburg Bar. She is very educated.'

'Oh! Is that so? I thought I recognised her,' I said. 'My case is in 2D at two o'clock. I just forgot to collect this document.'

'Look in the ledgers here on the counter if you don't mind. Here is the form. Just fill in all the necessary information and give it back to me,' he said, handing me the form.

That was the opportunity that I needed. I wanted to go through all the names in the ledger. Carefully, I studied the names from the current month of July and found nothing similar to my surname. *But I can just grab any name here and tell the dean it was the cousin that I talked about?* I played with the idea in my mind. *No, let me not complicate the matter.* I turned to June and found nothing there. There was nothing in May either. I began to panic. In April I anxiously moved my finger down the list; I found nothing on the first page, but turning to the second page my eye settled on the name Josephine Ntokozo Njomane. Next to it was the reference number 94/47778.

'Are you winning there?' asked the clerk, pausing to glance at me momentarily.

'I found it,' I said.

'Just fill in that form and let me sign it.'

I studied the form and nowhere on it was a space for my signature or name. All I had to fill in was the deceased's name, date of birth, when she passed away and the reference number. I gave the clerk the completed form and without even looking he signed it.

'Take it to room 4A and they will give you a certificate. You'll be required to pay six rand per certificate. Do you have any money on you?'

'Yes,' I said.

'Make sure that you have the right change. People are turned away all the time because the office doesn't have change.'

'Thanks for the advice, man.'

I only had two twenty rand notes, so I went outside to buy something, just to get some change before I entered room 4A. From the vendor outside on the pavement I bought a can of Coke and a hotdog. I asked for a plastic bag and the kind of change I wanted. Inside the building again, I went back to the clerk, who was busy helping an old woman.

'Man. This is for you and thanks for the assistance,' I said, giving the clerk the can of Coke and the hotdog.

'Thanks very much.'

'You're welcome. My name is Dingz,' I said, stretching out my hand for a handshake.

'I'm Tshepo.'

Inside room 4A there was another long queue. People sat on benches waiting for their names to be called. As I entered I saw that an albino guy was collecting all the papers from the clerk and passing them to a white man behind a fenced counter. The white man called out the names on the certificates after scrawling something on a piece of a paper. Those who went to collect the papers paid their money first before he gave them the signed certificates.

'Josephine Ntokozo Njomane,' called the white man.

I went to the counter as soon as the name was called.

'Six rand please.'

The money was ready inside my jacket pocket and I gave it to him. I took the small piece of a paper and read it as I left the office. The deceased had died of TB on the 17th of April; that was the only thing of note on that death certificate. I was still occupied with the privacy of my thoughts when I heard somebody calling my name.

'Bra Dingz.' I looked back. 'Did you manage to get the certificate?' It was the clerk – I had already forgotten his name.

'Sure. Thanks, my bra.'

'Do you have some skuif to spare, man?'

'I'll organize some just now. I don't have any with me.'

'I'm taking my lunch anyway; I might as well walk with you.'

I glanced at the long queue next to his counter. Everyone looked at him with disgust as he left them standing there without saying a word.

Outside I bought two packets of cigarettes, a pack of Consulate and a pack of Peter Stuyvesant. I gave him the pack of Consulate; he thanked me profusely and without my invitation promised to come to room 2D of the High Court to listen to my case if he got a chance at three. I made him feel welcome; after all, the money that I had used to buy him lunch and cigarettes was supposed to be his bribe, and the rest of it was now safe inside my wallet.

On the way to Wits I found an Internet café and made two copies of the death certificate. In a telephone booth nearby I tried to contact Dunga, but he wasn't in the office. I left a message with a guy who happened to answer the phone. At the De Korte Street Post Office I got my copies certified and walked to Wits University a happy man.

twenty-six

I looked at the dean with disbelief as the silence simmered between us. He examined the death certificate that I had submitted for a few seconds, as with his short, thick fingers he repeatedly stroked his bushy beard and drooping mustache.

He shoved the death certificate back at me. I could tell that he was not interested in my story and I began to chew my fingernails nervously. He ignored me and impatiently drummed his Parker pen against the desk as if he had discovered that the certificate in front of him was a fake. I tried as hard as possible to look as if I was grieving.

About six minutes had passed and, strangely, still no word had been spoken between us. The telephone, which was almost covered by the avalanche of papers on the table, rang. He looked at me and excused himself to answer it. I studied him, wondering anxiously what was on his mind concerning the death certificate.

He strummed at the keyboard of his computer as he talked to the person on the other end of the line. Meanwhile I was busy investigating the small library inside his office; judging from his collection of books he was a learned fellow.

The dean finished talking on the phone and put the receiver down. Without talking to me he raised himself from the chair and walked towards the bookshelf that stood against one of the white walls. He took out a book and came back to the desk with it.

Before he sat down he stared outside through the closed window for a second, as if he saw somebody he knew in the group of people that was about to enter the Oliver Schreiner law school building. Finally he looked away and sat down. The bottom drawer of his desk was already open; he picked out a large brown envelope and shoved the book inside.

'So, do you want to explain why you didn't submit this certificate in time, as we asked you to?'

'Well, ah . . .' I hesitated. 'It's because according to our culture I'm not supposed to touch anything connected with the deceased. And since it is taboo, I had to get permission from the elders.'

'What do you mean by saying a death certificate is taboo?'

I felt bile rise up my throat. 'I mean, if I touch anything of the deceased before such time as declared by the elders, I will be bringing bad luck to my family and myself.'

'What kind of bad luck?'

And what kind of a question is that? I asked myself.

'Any kind,' I replied, trying to keep calm.

'So why didn't you ask one of the elders of your family to contact the university?'

'I thought about that, but the person responsible for notifying everybody about the proceedings relating to the funeral was my uncle, and unfortunately he was very busy with more important arrangements.'

'So would you like to tell me why the dates do not correspond? Because this person died on the 17th of April, long before the exams were written.'

I was expecting that question and was prepared for it. 'That's because the deceased went missing some time ago and was only found at a government mortuary as I was writing my exams; fortunately before a state pauper funeral could be arranged. We couldn't bury her immediately without letting our relatives know of the arrangements. We are a very communal people, and so, even though the corpse had decomposed, we still had to agree as a family about the funeral arrangements,' I explained, trying to put the dean as far into his corner of white ignorance as possible

His dark eyes were studying my face.

'Is that so?'

'Yes.'

'But you know we heard the last application for a deferred

exam on Friday. You should have called in to arrange a meeting with us. Right now there is nothing we can do.'

Those words were unexpected after everything I had gone through to procure that death certificate.

'But Prof, I know for sure that there is something you can do if you want to. I mean . . .' I paused and shrugged my shoulders. 'You are the dean of the faculty, with the powers to make an exception in a case like this.'

'I'm sorry to say this, but, as I said to you before, we would be opening the floodgates for people to approach us with all kinds of stories after absconding from their exams.'

With mock anger, I snapped, 'Are you implying that I'm lying about my family bereavement?'

'No-no-no. Don't get me wrong. All I'm saying is that it is unbelievable that someone might die today and be buried three months later.'

'Meaning that blacks always lie about their situation?'

'I beg you not to put your words in my mouth.'

I studied the dean as, with agitation, he tapped his skull with his forefinger. I guessed he had read the malice that lay behind my words. I didn't care about the deferred exam any more; I wanted compensation for the time that I had wasted unnecessarily trying to get the death certificate. Most of all I was disturbed by the arrogance that he was showing about black people. I never thought that a man of his calibre would be so ignorant about the cancer of poverty that cripples so many families. Poverty means that you cannot give your loved one a proper burial. It also means that you cannot contact your relatives who live far away in times of need. Without money your children don't go to school like other kids. In a nutshell it means that you do not exist and you are wasted.

Although I had produced a sham certificate, I was angry that the dean was talking arrogantly to me. I didn't feel sorry that I lied to get it. Lying to get a death certificate was a practical affair to me. My world at that moment was simple – no lie, no certificate, no exam, no degree and back to the township, as simple as that. *What was the difference?* I asked myself disgustedly. *Mine was a sham certificate, but some white students, like Paul and Nikki, were permitted to write a deferred exam with trivial and frivolous aegrotats.*

I looked at the dean again. I was struggling to hide my anger. I gasped.

'I think you are prejudiced against me and there is no cure for that prejudice. I will have to contact the SRC to come and give you some lessons about our diverse cultures.'

'What makes you think that?'

'I can tell by the way you talk to me.'

'Let's not be emotional here. It's not that I'm denying that you are telling the truth, but we have to follow the rules.'

'Those rules, I think, must also take cognisance of the cultural diversity in this country. If they don't, they only apply arbitrarily to some of us.'

'I think we're not making any progress with this debate. What I suggest is that I'll put the matter forward during the staff meeting tomorrow morning and we'll let you know of the outcome by Friday at the latest. But I'm not promising anything,' concluded the dean, scratching his bald head with his finger.

I left the dean's office on that cold Monday afternoon with some hope, happy that I had at least pressurised him as far as I could. The following Thursday I received a letter from the faculty saying that I had been granted a deferred examination. The letter said that I would sit the exam in the first week of the third quarter when the university reopened from the mid-year recess. I was happy that I had succeeded and thanked Dunga for all his efforts.

twenty-seven

The 16th of December was born under overcast heavens. The university was closed for the academic year. All my friends had managed the minimum requirement to be re-admitted, although we had all failed one or two courses, except Theks who had done really well. I had failed two courses: Introduction to South African Law and Philosophy. But all of us were happy to graduate from our first year, shed our fresher nametags and become second-year students. To celebrate our achievements, we had agreed to meet at our usual hangout, the Dropout bar in Braamfontein.

Outside, a gust of wind lashed the rain that was hurled from the dark clouds above against the windows of the bar. As *Burn Out* by Sipho Mabuse stopped playing on the jukebox, I could hear the music of the rain drumming on the roof above. Through the haze of cigarette smoke I could see Themba selecting a jam on the jukebox. The song happened to be the favourite of most of the people inside and everybody sang along to Sharon Dee:

> Everybody say pa-rty
> Pa-rty
> Ye, ye, local is lekker
> Local is lekker
> Hey DJ, will you sing that song for me?
> Hey DJ, will you pump that song for me?

For the first time I had taken Nkanyi along with me to the bar. She was busy eating a large plate of chips. I looked outside and saw a red double-decker bus come to a halt at the bus stop next to the OK. It was quarter past eight and that was the last bus to the CBD.

212

Earlier that day I had meant to go to the rally at the FNB Stadium where President Mandela was going to speak. I was very disappointed to learn that it was cancelled due to the heavy rain.

'Shit, today's weather has disturbed so many important things,' I grumbled.

'Ag man, away with politics,' moaned Themba. 'His speech would have been the same old rhetoric of reconciliation.'

'People of South Africa,' started Dworkin, mimicking President Mandela's faltering voice, 'we must live together, black and white, in this land of ours. You must not fight. When conflict arises. Let us go to the negotiation table. We will find solutions. Like Mr De Klerk and myself did in CODESA. We shook hands. I thank you.'

There was a short burst of laughter around our table as Dworkin finished.

'I hate the fact that Dingane's Day has been changed into Day of Reconciliation with this absurd post-apartheid renaming,' continued Dworkin.

'But there's a good reason behind changing Dingane's Day to Reconciliation Day,' said Theks.

'No, no, no, no,' Dworkin shook his head slowly, 'this renaming is totally blotting out our history. Instead of thinking about King Dingane fighting the British, we now think of reconciliation with the same enemy who killed him.'

'But isn't that what we need in the present South African context?' asked Babes. 'We cannot afford another war of hatred. We are tired and need peace and unity.'

'That's liberal lightweight politics. It's time that we were proud of our history,' retorted Dworkin.

A song by Mahlathini and Mahotella Queens, *Gazette*, started playing on the jukebox. Nkanyi pushed her plate of chips aside and started singing along. She sipped her glass of Redds cider. I looked at her and she smiled. She wasn't used to my group of friends; the only person that she knew was Themba because he was going out with her friend.

'But I think the present name is best because there are no ambiguities about it,' I tried to reason. 'When this holiday was called Dingane's Day blacks and whites celebrated it differently. On the one hand whites celebrated their bravery in defeating Dingane. They dedicated this day to Dingane in order to fool black people into believing that the contribution that their troublesome hero had made to the history of South Africa was being honoured. The paradox was that as whites celebrated the death of the troublesome "kaffir king",' I gestured with my fingers to indicate inverted commas, 'blacks mourned his death.'

Dworkin's eyebrows lifted and his nostrils twitched as if he was registering the greatest shock of his life.

'I'm sorry to say this in front of your girlfriend, but I have to say it, my friend. You know what I think about you? I think you have become Witsified. Studying in this liberal institution has turned you into a typical example of the product of our historic abortion,' snapped Dworkin, his voice full of disbelief. 'How dare you speak of our king like that? I don't blame you, of course. I blame the power of the liberal education, which has poisoned your mind and made you use the language of the exploiters and call our king such a derogatory name. My broer, I think you need a brain transplant.'

Nkanyi was laughing at me and I felt embarrassed.

Themba took Dworkin's side. 'I think Dwork is right. Take Sharpeville Day for instance,' said Themba, blowing cigarette smoke out through his nose. 'On that day we used to commemorate the ruthless massacre of sixty-nine unarmed black men and women who protested against the notorious pass laws of apartheid on the 21st of March, 1961. The coming generation will have no idea why that day is a holiday, because it is now called Human Rights Day. That is like undermining the struggle of the black people in this country. And for what?' Themba asked. 'So that we can please the white people?'

I was quiet now. Nobody seemed to be siding with me. As I looked outside through the misty window, my eyes became glued

214

to the uninteresting sight of a man crossing Jorissen Street. He was running hard, trying to hide from the heavy rain. The man's trousers were wrapped against his legs due to the pressure of the wind. He tried to hide under the roof of the Standard Bank building opposite the bar but found no shelter there. He then crossed again to the safer side of the street. Soaked with the rain, the man entered the bar and paced around. Suddenly he smiled as he caught sight of Babes. As he walked towards our table I recognised him as the beggar we called Stomachache.

About a week ago Stomachache – he would always ask for money with his left hand pointing at his aching stomach – had confided in Babes that December the 16th was his birthday. Babes had promised to make Stomachache's day special. She had asked all of her male friends to donate their old clothes, not mentioning that she was going to donate them to Stomachache. Themba, T-Man, Mohammed, Dworkin, Dunga and myself all contributed our old rags. Meanwhile Babes had agreed with Stomachache to meet her at the bar to collect his birthday gift.

As he entered the bar, Babes had deliberately ignored him, pretending that they had no appointment, but she had two plastic bags full of clothes on her lap.

'Stomachache, what are you doing here?' asked Babes.

'Ha, sister! It's my birthday today and I'm hungry. Can you buy me a packet of chips please?' he answered, pointing at his stomach as usual.

'Wow, it's your birthday! People, let's sing a happy birthday song for him,' said Theks, smiling.

'Please, please don't sing for me,' pleaded Stomachache. 'That evil white skull over there hates my guts,' he whispered, pointing at the owner of the bar.

'I don't have money. You know I'm just a student. But I've got you a parcel,' said Babes, handing the two plastic bags to Stomachache. With a smile Stomachache thanked her and immediately went to the toilet to change. He came back disguised in a pair of

Dunga's old Levi jeans, my yellow T-shirt, T-man's running shoes and Themba's cap and jacket.

'Thank you, sister,' he said to Babes. 'One last request for my birthday – please give me five rand to buy some bread and chips as well. I'm very hungry, sister.'

'I'm completely broke. Ask my friends. Maybe they have something for you?' answered Babes, looking at Themba.

'No, don't look at me,' protested Themba, raising his hands. 'You know that it's not month end and I haven't been paid my salary yet. As they say, a salary is like a woman's period. It comes once a month and disappears within four days. I have nothing, my sister.'

There was a short burst of laughter.

'Ask them for me, please,' insisted Stomachache.

'Ehh! Do it yourself.'

'Please majita nabo sisi, please, please, please, please. Buy me packet chips please?' pleaded Stomachache earnestly.

Mohammed groped inside his pocket and gave Stomachache a five rand coin.

'You can finish these chips and the roll here,' offered Nkanyi.

As Stomachache was about to help himself to the chips and the roll, the bartender came and shoved him away. Stomachache lurched backwards and landed heavily against the pool table behind him.

'I warned you not to come here again and bother my customers, you scumbag,' growled the bartender angrily.

'Sorry, ngamla.'

'Now get the fuck out of my bar before I call the police.'

Stomachache got up and slowly walked to the other side of the table. Stretching out his hand, he took the plate with the chips and the roll and as fast as a lightning emptied it into his jacket pocket and scuttled out of the bar into the rain. The bartender laughed and apologised to us.

'Sorry about that.'

'Don't worry, we actually gave the food to him,' replied Babes.

'Can we have six more?' said T-Man to the bartender, flashing a fifty rand note.

'Coming just now,' he replied, collecting the two plates and four empty bottles from our table.

'Hey! Where do you know Stomachache from?' asked Themba, sniggering. 'He seems to have the hots for you, babe.'

Babes clicked her tongue. 'Who doesn't know Stomachache?' she answered protectively. 'I mean, he's always in this place, asking for money.'

'But yours looked like a special kind of relationship,' said Themba.

'Fuck you. What do you mean? You think I fuck him? I'm not mad.'

'Why not?' asked Themba, shrugging his shoulders. 'Who knows? Maybe your dildo is worn out and you want flesh?'

'Mind your language, boy, when speaking to your sister,' warned Theks.

'I'm available if you want it tonight. Please don't go to Stomachache because he will give you sextuplet even if you use a condom,' Themba finished contemptuously.

'I would rather use a cucumber than do it with you,' said Babes.

'You're very stingy with your thing, hey?'

'Even if we were the last two people on earth I wouldn't do it with you.'

'And what if it was you and Stomachache?'

'I would consider it, because he's more attractive than you.'

'I told you guys she has the hots for him, didn't I?' concluded Themba.

'Anyway. For your information I know Stomachache through my sister. He used to be her classmate before he dropped out of Wits.'

'Liar! Why would he be a beggar then?' questioned Dworkin.

Theks shook her head. 'You think it's easy out there in the real

217

world, don't you? But that's because we are protected by these varsity walls. Once we are let loose in the real world you'll realise that life is a matter of dog eat dog.'

'According to my sis, that guy was financially excluded in the second year of his B.Com,' said Babes.

'What's your sis doing now?' asked Dwork with great interest.

'She graduated six years ago and now she's a consultant at Deloitte.'

'Is she beautiful and fuckable?' Themba asked.

'Fuckoff! She told me about Stomachache when she was here three weeks ago. She was buying me some lunch at Steers when we came across him and he asked her for some money.'

'Was that your sis I saw you with the other day?' asked T-Man.

'Oh yeah. I forgot you saw me.'

Dworkin shook his head disapprovingly. 'I don't think I could live like Stomachache if I was excluded from varsity. I mean, come on people, I would be embarrassed to be a beggar right next to the varsity that excluded me.'

'You never know. Never say never,' warned Babes.

'I mean, unless I am bewitched and it's beyond my control or something.'

'We don't always choose our destinations,' added Babes.

Themba nodded his approval. 'I think Babes is right. You know, the unemployment rate is very high in this country even amongst those who have tertiary qualifications.

'Ja, you know the expectations our families have when we are still studying. Our unemployed siblings and retrenched parents expect us to graduate and make big changes to our appalling family conditions. And if we fail to fulfil those expectations, the frustration will pile up in our hearts and the weaker of us will become drunkards or even resort to crime,' reasoned Babes.

'But who said that education betters your life, anyway?' I asked.

'Who knows, maybe our drinking habits here at varsity are a taste of things to come,' said Babes.

'Spare me that ill prophecy. Nothing like that is going to happen,' said Dworkin. 'I'm going to be a lawyer and that's all.'

'It is the struggle of the black man everywhere in the world; to rise above our situation,' said T-Man.

'People, atrocities are not happening only here in South Africa, but everywhere, including Ethiopia where I come from,' blurted Mohammed. He spoke haltingly like a man searching for words. Throughout the night he had hardly opened his mouth except to sip his Coca-Cola.

'The struggle still continues even today, even here at the so-called liberal institutions,' I added, trying to change the topic.

'Of course. Look at the intake of black students,' added Dworkin.

'I always thought there were a reasonable number of black students at this varsity,' said T-man.

Dworkin and I exchanged a grumble of denial.

'Why? Because you see a lot of black faces here? Let me tell you something, my bra,' snapped Dworkin. 'The student intake in this varsity and elsewhere must reflect the demographic of this country. But that is not the case. Just because this white institution has opened its doors to attract more blacks does not necessarily mean that they are interested in improving our lives. The question is, how many black students are studying for professional degrees that will land them a good job at the end of the day?'

Dworkin looked around and waited for someone to challenge his point.

The bartender came and collected the empty bottles from our table. 'Give us five more, two Cokes, and a Redds for the lady here,' I said, handing the barman a fifty rand note.

'Coming right now,' said the barman as he walked away with the empty bottles.

'Yeah, guys,' sighed Dworkin, 'the intake of black students in this varsity is really questionable. I'm not being xenophobic here,' he said, looking guilty, 'but just look at the majority of black stu-

219

dents in this varsity and tell me if they are South Africans?' he paused and took a drag on his cigarette. He blew smoke out through his nose and continued. 'I'm telling you that the majority of black students come here from outside this Mzantsi Africa. They are used as window dressing to fool the South African public, so that when they look, they think that the varsity is adhering to the affirmative action programme.'

There was a little pause in the conversation as the barman arrived, carrying our order on a tray. He put the drinks on the table and gave me my change. I didn't give him a tip, just put my change in my pocket.

'I think you're forgetting one thing, comrade,' I said, as I started pouring Redds cider into Nkanyi's glass, 'and that's the fact that an institution like this one is run like a corporation, where vice-chancellors are like CEOs, academics are like managers and students like me and you are the customers.' Themba handed me a beer and I poured it into my glass. 'Students from foreign soil are seen as reliable customers because they pay hard cash towards their academic fees.' I took a sip of my beer. 'But we are bad news for the varsity because we end up owing money to it at the end of each academic year, and may even get financially excluded like Stomachache. That is why institutions like this one remain ivory towers to black South Africans.'

Babes nodded her approval. 'Absolutely. You're right. These guys from outside South Africa are sponsored by their governments while studying here. That is why their studies go so smoothly.' She stretched her long arm to emphasise the word smooth. 'Because they have nothing to worry about. Look at the so-called traditionally black campuses.' She flung both her hands out and opened her eyes wide. 'The reason they are threatening to close down is that they cater for the impoverished black masses; they cannot maintain themselves without financial help from the government.'

Dworkin shrugged his shoulders and took a sip from his glass. 'Indeed, how many black lecturers or professors do we have here in this varsity?' he asked. 'And how many of those, if any, are South Africans? The institution itself is afraid that if it increases the intake of black student and academics, it will be accused of compromising its academic standards and might lose out financially.'

'I think you're right,' said Theks, 'I think of all the black lecturers in the law faculty only two or three are South Africans. The rest are from outside.'

T-man, who had been a bit quiet, shook his head. 'You guys must stop your racist remarks. Do you see how black foreigners are treated in your country? You guys forget very easily how you were supported and given asylum when fighting for democracy. Now you fail to return that favour.' He stopped and scratched a pimple on his chin.

Dworkin wasn't convinced. 'But the situation is very different, because I was told by some guys who were in exile in Lusaka that they were living in designated camps. They didn't roam around like these guys are doing here.'

Theks nodded her approval. 'Yeah, he's right. And again, our reasons were more political than economic, unlike most of the foreigners who are staying here in South Africa. Look at the Nigerians who are selling drugs to small kids on the streets.'

'Are you sure that the Nigerians are the ones who are doing such things, or it is just an allegation by your xenophobic media?' You guys here in South Africa must not only concentrate on the negative aspects about foreigners,' riposted T-Man.

Babes shook her head disapprovingly. 'Thank you very much, but we can't afford to harbour the worst criminals in the name of an African Renaissance, these people are just holding our country to ransom.'

The music from the jukebox interrupted us. Themba got up on his feet to sing along to like that old song by Peter Frampton.

'Do you feel like I do?' he shouted for everyone inside to hear.

'Yes!' we all shouted after him.

Then Themba changed the lyrics of the song:

'Are you drunk like I'm drunk?' he shouted.

'Yeah, that's true,' we all shouted except Mohammed and my shy Nkanyi.

'Oh, that's true. But that's not right. That's not right. That's not right.' finished Themba.

We were all drunk.

Twenty minutes later Themba had fallen asleep on his chair. The jukebox was off and the bar was quiet. Themba's anal brakes failed him and he fired a long, loud anal explosion. Theks's laughter woke him up. 'Uhh, sis! That's beneath your dignity, boy.'

Embarrassed, Themba looked outside where dawn was spreading slowly.

'That's nature. You can't stop the force of nature,' I said protectively.

'You should at least try in a public place like this,' said Babes.

I looked at the time. It was half past four in the morning. The rain had long stopped drumming in the street outside and there were only few people left in the bar. The bartender rang the bell and shouted, 'Last round, guys. The bar is closing in thirty minutes.'

'I think we better leave, it's late now,' said Babes to all of us.

The three of us – Dworkin, Themba and myself – were going to sleep in Dworkin's room at the Y. Themba had to start work at eight that morning. I had arranged for Nkanyi to sleep at Babes's place.

'I told you that you were an amateur. You can't compete with the drinking heavyweights, boy,' said Babes to Themba.

'Next time we should mix his beer with water so that he doesn't get drunk and embarrass us in public,' added Theks.

We were out.

The author wishes to acknowledge that snippets of the following songs have been used in the novel:

'Don't Give Up', written and performed by Peter Gabriel (p. 10); 'Ding Dong', written and performed by Joe Nina (p. 77); 'iStokvel', written by Manqoba Ntobela and performed by Woza Africa (p. 83); 'It's About Time', written and performed by Boom Shaka (pp. 100 and 198); 'Local is Lekker' performed by Sharon Dlamini (p. 212); and 'Do You Feel Like We Do' written and performed by Peter Frampton (p. 221).